Avery in his arms...

The memory was all he could handle.

She got to him on so many levels. Him, the original user. The guy who'd used his unmistakable charm to fake his way to a pedigree no one questioned. He was immune to the vulnerable; he'd trained himself to be. Because Marcus Price never took his eye off the prize, and he was always prepared to work hard to get whatever he wanted.

You want Avery Cullen.

Sure, he wanted Avery. She was a goddess, with a body that promised untold sexual delight, yet she maintained an air of naivety, of untapped raw passion, that was enough to entice even the most jaded of souls.

But there was something he wanted even more....

THE HIGHEST BIDDER

At this high-stakes auction house where everything is for sale, true love is priceless.

Don't miss a single story in this new continuity!

GILDED SECRETS by Maureen Child
EXQUISITE ACQUISITIONS by Charlene Sands
A SILKEN SEDUCTION by Yvonne Lindsay
A PRECIOUS INHERITANCE by Paula Roe
THE ROGUE'S FORTUNE by Cat Schield
GOLDEN BETRAYALS by Barbara Dunlop

A SILKEN SEDUCTION

BY
YVONNE LINDSAY

First published in Great Britain 2013
by Mills & Boon, an imprint of Harlequin (UK) Limited.
Harlequin (UK) Limited, Eton House, 18-24 Paradise Road,
Richmond, Surrey TW9 1SR

© Harlequin Books S.A. 2012

ISBN: 978 0 263 90046 0

Special thanks and acknowledgement to Yvonne Lindsay for her contribution to *The Highest Bidder* miniseries.

Harlequin (UK) policy is to use papers that are natural, renewable and recyclable products and made from wood grown in sustainable forests. The logging and manufacturing process conform to the legal environmental regulations of the country of origin.

Printed and bound in Spain
by Blackprint CPI, Barcelona

New Zealand born, to Dutch immigrant parents, **Yvonne Lindsay** became an avid romance reader at the age of thirteen. Now, married to her 'blind date' and with two fabulous children, she remains a firm believer in the power of romance. Yvonne feels privileged to be able to bring to her readers the stories of her heart. In her spare time, when not writing, she can be found with her nose firmly in a book, reliving the power of love in all walks of life.

She can be contacted via her website:
www.yvonnelindsay.com

Recent titles by the same author:

ONE SECRET NIGHT *(The Master Vintners)*
A FATHER'S SECRET *(Billionaires and Babies)*
A FORBIDDEN AFFAIR *(The Master Vintners)*
THE WAYWARD SON *(The Master Vintners)*

Did you know these are also available as eBooks?
Visit www.millsandboon.co.uk

To my fellow authors—Maureen, Charlene, Paula, Cat and Barbara. It's been a genuine pleasure, thank you.

And, to CG and JA—
working with you guys is always a delight.

One

"Miss Cullen is *not* taking visitors!"

Avery started at the outraged voice of her housekeeper—the action making her blotch a daub of the yew-green paint at the end of her brush. The sound of footsteps came swiftly on the ancient paved path behind her. She sighed and put the paintbrush down. On this overcast and suddenly autumnal London day she was already losing the light and, interruptions aside, the painting wasn't going well anyway. *If only passion for a subject made up for a lack of everything else,* she thought as she reached for the linseed-oil-scented rag on the shelf of her easel and wiped her hands before turning to see what the fuss was about.

Her housekeeper usually had no trouble heading off visitors at the front door. The woman was fiercely protective of Avery and fully respected the younger woman's wish for privacy. But it seemed someone had managed to cut past Mrs. Jackson's normally effective defense. The man walking a clear yard ahead of the stout housekeeper had his eyes on only one thing. Avery.

Tall, with dark blond hair that, while short, managed to look like he'd just rolled out of bed, and a light beard that suggested he hadn't shaved in a couple of days, there was no doubt he was disreputably good-looking. There was also something vaguely familiar about him. No, surely not. She would have remembered meeting him before. She didn't know him at all. *Sure you do,* a tiny voice whispered from deep inside. *Wasn't he that guy Macy had pointed out when they were in New York for the Tarlington auction?* Avery shoved the voice back down where it belonged as a shiver of something undefined shimmered up her neck. Not fear. Not even apprehension over the stranger striding so determinedly toward her, strangely enough.

No, this was something else. Something she had about as much trouble putting a name to as she'd had capturing the beauty of her father's favorite garden in oils on canvas. Whatever it was, it made a bloom of heat kiss her cheeks and she felt her pulse rate lift a notch. Irritation at being disturbed, she told herself, but she knew it was anything but.

"I'm sorry, Miss Cullen, I informed Mr. Price you aren't taking visitors but he just wouldn't listen." Disapproval was clear in every vowel of the housekeeper's London East End origins. She gave an indignant sniff. "He *says* he has an appointment."

Mrs. Jackson's rosy cheeks glowed even brighter than usual at this clear invasion of her mistress's privacy.

"It's all right, Mrs. Jackson. He's here now," Avery answered as soothingly as she could and, summoning the hospitality that had been drummed into her from an early age, she offered, "perhaps our guest might like some tea on the terrace before he leaves?"

"Coffee, please, if you have it," the man said, his voice

pure Boston Brahmin all the way, but it was his name that finally filtered through her memory and caught her attention.

As Mrs. Jackson bustled off to prepare the coffee, still bristling with outrage and muttering under her breath, Avery gave him her full consideration.

"Price? So you'd be Marcus Price, of Waverly's in New York?" she asked.

Waverly's was the auction house that had handled her friend Macy's mother's estate sale. Seeing what Macy had gone through over the sale had made Avery all the more determined to hold on to the treasures that made up her past—whether she liked them or not. At least she had the luxury, literally, of not having to sell those memories as poor Macy had.

"I'm flattered you remember my name," he said with an easy smile that made her stomach do an uncomfortable flip in response.

"Don't be," she answered in as quelling a tone as she could muster, given the unbidden buzz of heat that unfurled through her body at his nearness. "I made my position on the sale of my father's Impressionist collection quite clear when you first contacted me. You've come a long way for a wasted journey."

He smiled in response and a flutter of unadulterated feminine interest flickered through her veins. A flutter she attempted to suppress as rapidly as it arose. As handsome as he was, and he certainly was that, she knew his type all too well. Bold, brash, confident. He was everything she wasn't and he was in for a disappointment if he thought she would be talked into selling her late father's much-coveted collection.

"Now I've finally had the chance to meet you, I know my time wasn't entirely wasted."

His voice was laden with innuendo and the surety he would get what he came for.

"You can stop trying to flatter me, Mr. Price. Better men than you have tried…and failed."

"Marcus, please."

She nodded, a bare ascension of her head. "Marcus, then. It doesn't change anything. I'm not selling and I really don't understand why you're here."

"Your assistant, David Hurley, arranged our meeting two weeks ago. I had assumed he'd told you but—" his green eyes narrowed as he obviously noted the flash of anger that she knew must show across her expressive features "—I can see from your expression that he neglected to do so. I'm sorry, Miss Cullen. I believed you were open to discussions."

Oh, he was good. Charming, sincere—she could almost believe him if she didn't wonder just how much he'd bribed David to set this up. She would have hoped her late father's assistant was above such a thing but apparently not. And, to be honest, she couldn't imagine any other way Marcus would have succeeded in getting the appointment he'd been hounding her for in the past month. She made a mental note to follow up with David as soon as possible. He was still based in her hometown of Los Angeles and despite the years of service he'd given her dad, if he didn't have a valid explanation, she was prepared to lose him over this. Trust was something earned and, when breached, easily broken.

"Your coffee should be ready," Avery answered, refusing to confirm or deny David's part in this. "Shall we go up to the terrace?"

"Thank you." Marcus held out one hand, gesturing for her to precede him.

She couldn't help but feel the assessment of his eyes on her back as she followed the path that led to the terrace at the side of the house. Every feminine cell in her body wished she was wearing something more.... Well, *anything* other than the old jeans and T-shirt she'd chosen to wear for painting today. In the instant she thought it, she dashed the vanity from her mind. She wasn't out to impress Marcus Price or anyone like him. She'd learned the hard way how to read people who wanted to use her for their own advancement and she had no doubt that securing the Cullen Collection, the Impressionist paintings her father had acquired over the past two and a half decades, would be a golden feather in this hotshot's career-advancement cap.

They arrived on the terrace just as Mrs. Jackson wheeled out a cart laden with afternoon tea—or coffee as the case was—and transferred the cups and saucers to a small wrought-iron table set with two matching chairs. Avery invited Marcus to sit down.

"Cream or milk?" Avery asked as she finished pouring the aromatic dark brew from the silver coffeepot embossed with the crest of her English mother's family.

"Just black, thanks."

"Sugar?" she continued, striving to follow the social graces her parents would have expected of her had they both still been alive.

"Two, please."

She arched a brow. "Two? Ah, yes, I can see why."

"You think I need sweetening?" There was a hint of laughter in his voice.

"You said it, not me."

Using silver tongs, she dropped two cubes of sugar in his coffee and handed the cup and saucer across to him.

"Thank you," he said, holding it in one hand while with the other he picked up the silver teaspoon resting on the saucer, to stir his coffee.

Avery found herself mesmerized. Long fingered, yet broad and capable, his hands were both those of an artist and a man more accustomed to physically working hard for a living. That traitorous curl of warmth licked through her body again. She really needed to get out more, she thought as she tried to quash the attraction she felt toward him. She'd been sequestered in her London home since her father's death and, aside from a brief trip to New York to support her best friend during the auction of Macy's famous mother's possessions, she'd kept social contact to an absolute minimum. Maybe it was time for that to change. In fact, hadn't Macy told her she should at least meet Marcus, if only for the eye-candy quotient?

Change or not, Marcus Price was too slick for someone like her.

"About the Cullen Collection—" he began after taking a sip of his coffee.

"I'm not interested in selling. I don't know how I can be any clearer on the subject," Avery interrupted.

She really was losing patience over this. She couldn't expect anyone to fully understand just why she was so determined to hold on to the paintings. They were collecting dust in her family's Los Angeles mansion. Deep down she knew she needed to do something—loan them to a museum or a gallery, anyone who'd appreciate them more than she did. But she couldn't bring herself to let them go just yet. Her father had amassed the Impressionist works over her lifetime and even as a child she'd understood his satisfaction in acquiring another piece for the collection.

Forrest Cullen had loved every canvas with a devotion Avery had often envied for herself. Oh, she knew her father had loved her in his own distant way, but even after her mother's death when she was five he'd continued to remain a disconnected parent. She'd always felt her father had had two great loves in his life. His wife and his collection. She wasn't about to part with the remaining tangible link she had to the man she'd idolized her whole life. It, and the garden here in London that he'd so patiently tended, made her feel closer to him—made his loss less raw.

Marcus interrupted her thoughts, bringing her very firmly into the present.

"I'm sure you're well aware of what the collection could command from the right buyers."

Avery gave him a cynical half smile. "Look around you, Marcus. I'm not exactly short of a dollar or two."

"Then think of it this way. Those paintings deserve to be in the hands and view of people who truly appreciate them."

She stiffened. Had David told him that she actually didn't even like most of the collection? No, surely even he didn't know that much.

"Are you suggesting I don't appreciate my father's collection? That's rather assumptive, wouldn't you say?"

Marcus narrowed his green eyes and gave her an assessing look. She fought the urge to tidy herself under his scrutiny, to smooth the wisps that, in the curse of fine blond hair, had escaped her ponytail and even now tickled against her cheeks in the light afternoon breeze.

"I'm sure you have your reasons, but I believe that anyone can be swayed with the right enticement."

She laughed aloud. The sheer audacity of the man.

"I'm not interested in enticement, Mr. Price," she said, deliberately returning to using the formal version of his name. "Now, if you've finished your coffee, I'll ask Mrs. Jackson to see you out."

"Are you going back to your painting?" he asked, not moving an inch from his seat.

She felt her guard rise even higher. "I believe I asked you to leave, Mr. Price."

"Marcus. And you did. Ever so nicely, but—" he leaned forward and traced one finger across a smear of paint on the index finger of her right hand "—I find myself wanting to continue to discuss art, and its many forms, with you."

For just a moment she was trapped in the thrall of his touch. So light, and yet pulling from deep within her a reaction so intense it took her breath clean away. If circumstances had been different, she'd lean toward him, too, and see whether he tasted as enticing as his words sounded.

The squawk of a bird settling in a nearby tree broke the

spell Marcus had woven. She wasn't into fleeting pleasure and a fling with Marcus Price would be exactly that. A fling. Life was worth so much more—correction, *she* was worth so much more than that. Avery pointedly looked at his hand before withdrawing her own from beneath it.

"Sadly, I can't say the same."

He quirked his lips in a half smile. "C'mon, I bet you're wondering, even now, what it is that you're doing wrong with your painting, why it's not working."

The challenge hung in the air between them.

"Wrong?" she answered, raising her brows.

"I am recognized as something of an expert in art, you know."

"Selling it, perhaps."

"Identifying what's worth selling," he corrected, his voice still light but carrying an underlying steel that proved she might have dented his pride just a little.

"So, tell me, what is it that I'm doing *wrong,*" she challenged. She didn't for one minute believe he'd be able to direct her any better than she could herself.

"It's in the way you've captured the light."

"The light?" Oh, God, she must sound like an idiot parroting his words.

"C'mon, I'll show you."

Before she could answer he'd risen from his chair and taken her hand in his own. The warmth of his fingers as they curled around hers, holding them lightly but without any hint of letting go anytime soon, felt oddly right. She was helpless to protest as he led her down the shallow terrace steps and back to where her easel stood waiting with its half-finished canvas.

"Actually, it's more in the way you haven't captured the light," Marcus said, pointing to the dappled texture of rich early autumnal tones on the stretched canvas. "See? Here, and here. Where's the light, the sun, the warmth? Where's it coming from? Where's the last caress of summer?"

In an instant she knew exactly what he was talking about and she mixed some paint on her palette and, with a clean brush, swiftly applied her attention to one area of the canvas.

"Like that?" she asked, stepping back.

"Yeah, just like that. You know what you're doing. How did you miss it?"

"I guess the light's been missing from my life for a while now," she said without thinking. "And, I stopped looking for it."

Two

Marcus couldn't help but feel the solid wall of her grief as he watched her. He acknowledged it and then swept it to the back of his mind, where he could potentially deal with it later. Right now he had to keep his advantage. He'd been plotting for months to get beyond Avery Cullen's well-trained guard dogs and he wasn't about to waste his gain now.

He was close, so close he could feel it in the tingling in the pit of his stomach. If he could secure the rights to sell the Cullen Collection, his bid to become a partner at Waverly's would be a foregone conclusion—and it would take him one almighty step closer to getting back that which belonged to his family.

"It's tough, losing a parent," he said, injecting the right note of sympathy into his voice.

She gave a brief nod and he glimpsed a sheen of moisture in her wide-spaced blue eyes before she turned away from him and added a few more touches to the painting. This was wrong. A gentleman wouldn't be capitalizing on her sorrow—

but he was no gentleman, certainly not by birth. But even though he knew what should be the right thing to do, he was so close to his goal he could almost taste the success. He saw her slender shoulders lift as she drew in a deep breath, then settle once more as she let it pass slowly through her lips.

"It's why this painting is so important to me. This garden was his favorite place in the world, especially in the fall. He always said he felt closest to my mother here. I take it you've lost a parent, too?" she asked, her voice a little shaky.

"Yeah, both of them."

It wasn't strictly true. While he had lost his mother before he could remember her, his father was still alive—somewhere. The man had stated his own price for staying out of Marcus's life—a price Marcus's grandfather had willingly paid—and surprisingly, so far, his father had kept his word.

Her voice was firmer when she spoke, her eyes filled with compassion. "I'm sorry, Marcus."

And he knew she was. He felt a pang of guilt that he should accept her sympathy. He hadn't known either of his parents. His mother had given birth to him while serving time for drug possession and supply, leaving him to the care of her father from the day he was born. She'd later died when he was about two years old, using the drugs that had ruled her life since her late teens—the price of the contraband eventually being far higher than she'd ever anticipated. His father had been itinerant, turning up only when he knew he could fleece the old man for more money in exchange for leaving Marcus alone. Eventually his grandfather had sold his dearest possession to buy his late daughter's partner off for good—that action had, strangely enough, led Marcus right here to Avery's garden.

He shrugged, determined to stay on track. He couldn't change who his parents were, but he could certainly make amends to his grandfather for the damage they'd wreaked on Grampa's life. And that started with getting back the painting the old man should never have been forced to sell.

"It was a long time ago, but thank you," he said, reaching out to rest one hand briefly on her shoulder and giving it a gentle squeeze.

He kept the touch light, not lingering too long, but the heat of her body through her T-shirt seared like a brand on his palm. He forced himself to let go and create a little more distance between them. He already knew she found him attractive. It had been there in the instinctive flare of her pupils, in the blush across her cheeks, in the way she kept checking him out even when she tried not to. He wasn't above using that to his advantage in this instance, but his own attraction to her left him more than a little startled.

He needed to return things to an even footing and he forced his concentration back toward her work.

"Landscapes aren't really your thing, are they?" he asked with sudden perspicacity.

"What makes you say that?" she asked. "You think it's no good? Seriously, if you're trying to get on my good side, you're going about it the wrong way."

He gave a short chuckle, giving in to the burst of humor her wry observation initiated.

"I didn't say it wasn't good. Technically, you're doing a great job, but a photo would serve just as well."

"Damned with faint praise," she said wryly, snapping the lid closed on her box of paints and gathering up her brushes and the small folding table she'd rested her supplies on.

"So what is your passion?" Marcus persisted. "What is it that really sets you on fire?"

She lifted her gaze to his face but her observation of him was different from how her eyes had skipped over his features before. This time, he sensed she wasn't looking at him as a man, but as a subject.

"Portraits," she said with a shrug, "nudes."

A bolt of sexual hunger rocked through him. Nudes? What would it be like to sit for her? he wondered. He rapidly ex-

tinguished the growing fire that lit through his veins. Miss
Avery Cullen was getting more and more interesting by the
second but he didn't want to scare her off. Not when there
was so much at stake.

"Like your great-great-uncle?" he asked.

She gave a careful nod. "You seem to know your stuff."

"Waverly's doesn't make a habit of hiring idiots," he replied.

"I'm sure it doesn't," she agreed as she continued to gather
her things together. "You know my uncle's work?"

"I studied him in college. Baxter Cullen's work has always
been among my favorites." He reached for her unfinished canvas and easel. "Here, let me help you with that."

"Thanks," she said, to his surprise. He hadn't expected
her to accept his offer. They started to walk back toward the
house. "Do you paint?"

"Not my strength, I'm afraid," he answered with complete honesty. "But I've always had an appreciation for well-
executed work."

She stopped at the double set of French doors that led into
the house. "I have a Baxter Cullen here, would you be interested in seeing it?"

For a second his heart skipped a beat. Was she referring to
Lovely Woman—the very painting he sought to restore to his
grandfather? He fought to inject the right note of interest, as
opposed to overwhelming desire, into his voice.

"That would be great, if you're sure it's no bother."

"It's no bother. Come up to my studio," Avery said.

He followed her through a well-used parlor and then up
the wide wooden staircase that led to the next floor. His feet
were silent on the carpet runner even while his heart beat a
tattoo in his chest he was almost certain had to be audible.
The second set of stairs was narrower, the handrail less or-
nate, but he could see the patina of time on the highly polished wood and wondered, with a tinge of bitterness, how

many generations of hands had taken their right to live here for granted. He'd lay odds no one in the Cullen family, or even on Avery's mother's side, had ever had to sell anything just to put food on the table.

You can take the boy out of the neighborhood, he could hear his grandfather's voice echoing in his mind, *but you can't take the neighborhood out of the boy.* Well, he'd spent most of his adult life working hard to try to prove Grampa wrong on that score. One day he'd be able to give them both what they deserved, and hopefully that one day, courtesy of Avery Cullen, would be soon.

"This was the nursery, back in the day when children were seen and not heard," Avery commented as she directed Marcus where to put the easel and painting and moved across the room to a set of sliding doors that, when opened, revealed a built-in bench and basin.

He looked around as she cleaned her brushes. The high unadorned ceilings reflected the cool light that streamed in from the tall windows. He could see why Avery used this room as a studio. But then his attention was caught by the very thing he sought.

Blood pounded in his ears as he approached the small but perfectly executed nude of a young woman bathing, and he fought to keep his breathing under control. He stopped in front of the picture and counted slowly backward from one hundred. His eyes drank in the vision in front of him. Technique aside, the rendering was near perfect. He almost felt like a voyeur, as if he'd caught a glimpse into the private life and time of the woman, as she dragged a dripping rag gracefully over one softly rounded shoulder.

A dreadful urge to simply rip the painting from its hook and race down the stairs and out of here bloomed inside. An urge he instinctively suppressed. He hadn't waited this long just to ruin everything now but it was harder than he'd expected to finally see the painting his grandfather had been forced to sell twenty-five years ago.

"It's beautiful, isn't it?" Avery said from behind him. "Apparently she was one of the maids in Baxter's household. There was a bit of a scandal over this back then. She was dismissed by Baxter's wife, Isobel, when she saw the painting. Isobel accused the maid of having an affair with Baxter and insisted her husband destroy the picture. Obviously he didn't. There was a rumor that he sent the painting to the maid, but we have no actual proof of who owned it after it left his house."

"Interesting that there was no blame laid at her husband's feet for exploiting a maid in his employment." As hard as he tried he couldn't keep a hint of bitterness from his voice. The underclass always bore more than its share of blame in situations like this.

Avery shrugged. "I don't know whether there was or not. His wife was apparently quite a forceful character. Probably necessary when Baxter was oblivious to everything but his work."

"And, no doubt, his subject."

A small smile tugged at her lips. "Yes," she conceded. "And his subject, although I wonder if he ever saw her as anything other than tones and light and shadows."

Marcus clenched his jaw to hold back the words that hovered on the tip of his tongue. It wouldn't do to let Avery know that he had no doubt that Baxter Cullen had most definitely seen his model as far, far more than that.

After all, the subject in question had been Marcus's own great-grandmother.

Marcus forced himself to shift the conversation away from the woman in the painting. Knowing it was because of him that the nude no longer hung on Grampa's sitting-room wall made seeing the work more emotional than he'd anticipated—and Marcus didn't do emotion.

"How did your father come into possession of *Lovely Woman*?"

"Through a broker, I imagine. That's how he bought most of his favorites, although he was pretty good at spotting bargains in estate lots and secondhand stores. Even so, he was a stickler for paying a fair price."

"I'm surprised you have it here in your studio."

"It's my inspiration," she answered simply.

"For your nudes?"

"Not just my work—for everything, really. It reminds me to look for beauty in all things, no matter what the circumstances."

"I'm surprised you have to look. Aren't you surrounded by beauty here in your home?" He tore his gaze from the painting and turned to face her.

Her full lips twisted in a wry smile. "You'd be surprised at what surrounds me and what's expected of me."

He could sense there was hurt lying behind her words, but surely living in her gilded world couldn't be all that bad? In the distance Marcus heard the sonorous chimes of a grandfather clock, counting out the hour. It was getting late. While every urge pushed him to press the advantage of her current openness he knew that underneath she was probably still as skittish as a first-time buyer at auction.

"I'd better head off," he said. "Thank you for showing me the painting."

"You're welcome. Here, let me show you back downstairs."

Avery led the way down the two flights of stairs and through to the black-and-white-tiled foyer. At the door, Marcus turned and put out his hand, surprised when, without hesitation, Avery took it in her smaller one.

"I'm not going to give up, you know," he warned her with a smile.

"Give up?"

"On getting you to agree to sell your father's collection."

Avery laughed, the intensity that had clouded her features while they were upstairs in the studio lifting with the sound. "It's not going to happen."

"I usually get what I want," he drawled, this time letting his gaze caress her face before sliding lower to where her pulse beat visibly at her neck.

A warm flush of color stained her skin and her fingers tightened on his imperceptibly before she withdrew them from his clasp.

"Perhaps it's time you learned to cope with disappointment," she said, her voice a little husky.

"You think I don't know disappointment?" he asked, injecting just the right amount of teasing into his tone.

She flushed again. "I'm sure it's not up to me to know that."

"I've had my share. It just served to make me more determined to get exactly what I want out of life."

"And is brokering the Cullen Collection what you want out of life?" she asked, lifting her chin a little in a silent challenge.

"It's at the top of my list at the moment," he acceded with a calculated smile. "But there are other things I want."

"I'm intrigued," Avery said, stepping back a little, as if creating more distance between them could overcome her curiosity. "Perhaps you could explain to me exactly why my father's paintings are so important to you over dinner here tonight? We dine at eight."

Satisfaction swelled inside him. It was like taking candy from a baby. She'd gone from emphatically saying "no" to now being interested, albeit remotely. It was an important first step. Now he had to make sure he left her feeling secure enough that she'd grant his request.

"I'd love to discuss it further over dinner, but not here. Why don't I take you out instead? I still need to check into my hotel but I can be back here in say—" he cast a glance at the wafer-slim Piaget timepiece on his wrist "—two hours. Does that suit you?"

For a moment he thought she might refuse, but then her face cleared and she gave him a small smile. "I haven't been out in a while, so, yes, I'd like that. I'll see you at seven?"

"I'll be here."

As Marcus made his way down the shallow concrete stairs that led from the front door toward where he'd parked his rental car, he fought to control the urge to fist pump the air in triumph. Every word, every second brought him closer to success. He could see the ink on his partnership offer already.

Three

Avery leaned back against the door after closing it behind Marcus. She couldn't believe she'd invited him to come back for dinner, let alone agreed to go out with him! He made her uncomfortable with his direct, impossibly green-eyed stare, and with his very reason for being here in London—hassling her about selling her father's collection. But for some bizarre reason he also lit an interest in her that she hadn't felt in a long time and she was intrigued to know why he was so intent on procuring the collection.

Surely it couldn't hurt to spend a few more hours in his company?

Two hours. She had two hours to get herself tidied up and in a presentable enough state to go out. She mentally ran through her wardrobe options. She'd left most of her party clothes back in Los Angeles but she had a few pieces that might work for tonight.

She sighed. Who was she kidding? He hadn't asked her out because he was attracted to her. He was probably more attracted to the commission he'd earn if she agreed to let him list the collection for sale. God, even thinking about it brought a sense of loss to throb painfully inside her chest.

She wasn't going to part with the collection, but that wouldn't stop her from making the most of Marcus Price's company. He had come across to her as being pretty astute about art and his reaction to *Lovely Woman* had surprised and intrigued her. He'd been enthralled by her ancestor's work. Baxter Cullen had been one of the most revered American painters of the early twentieth century; it stood to reason that Marcus would have studied him while in college. Yet she sensed there was something more about his interest in the painting up in her studio.

In fact, she thought as a shiver ran down her spine, he'd stared at the painting with almost the same avarice as when he'd stared at her in the gardens. As if he had a sole purpose to acquire a specific thing or, in her case, person.

The shiver rippled through her body again, but this time it had nothing to do with caution or anxiety and everything to do with instinctive female response to someone who was very definitely pure alpha all the way. She hadn't been this attracted to anyone in a very long time. It was frightening and exhilarating. It had been too long since she'd allowed herself to *feel*. With her father's sudden illness—well, sudden to her as he'd kept the truth of his cancer to himself for the better part of nine months—and subsequent death, she'd locked away her feelings. Focused her energy into doing everything she could to support her father during his last months here in London, putting everything in her life on hold.

She'd lost a great deal in that time. Her father, first and foremost, as the disease ravaged his body, then his mind, so that he barely recognized his surroundings anymore, let alone his daughter. And secondly, the group of people she'd called friends—friends who could probably better have been identified as sycophants, people only interested in what knowing her could gain for them. They'd all withdrawn from her. Never for a moment supporting her in her time of need. All except Macy, her one true friend, but there was only so much a person could do with an ocean between them.

It had been the withdrawal of her friends that had made her see how truly alone she was in this world. Sure, a few of them had contacted her after her father's obituary had appeared in the papers. But not to offer sympathy. Instead they'd asked her when she'd be back in circulation, making it painfully obvious that her financial contribution to their frequent partying had been missed now that they had to "slum it" at bad tables at restaurants, drink cheaper bottles of champagne and take cabs rather than limousines. How no one else's name had quite the pull that the Cullen name had. Avery had realized she'd let herself be used, all in the guise of being a part of something that was fun, carefree, connected.

When her eyes had opened it had been herself she looked at most critically. She'd let it happen, she'd allowed herself to be walked over and used for what she was, not who. In the weeks following her father's funeral she'd promised herself one thing—she would never allow herself to be used again. She'd withdrawn, wrapping herself in her grief and throwing herself into the arts-related charities her family had always supported—even toying with creating a new one of her own, one that would support children's aspirations in the artistic realms.

Avery pushed herself off the door and headed for the stairs. At least with Marcus Price she knew exactly what he wanted. The Cullen Collection and nothing else. Sure, he might pay her some compliments, make her feel like a woman with heated blood in her veins, but that was where it began and ended. He had an agenda. She was safe from hurt provided she went into this with her eyes wide open—and they were most definitely open.

* * *

Marcus pulled the classic Jaguar he'd rented to a halt at the top of the loop in the Cullen driveway. Anticipation thrummed through his body at the thought of the next few hours with Avery Cullen. She was wary, and justifiably so. He'd have to tread very carefully to get what he wanted but he had no doubt he'd succeed. Besides, spending the evening in her company would be nothing but pleasure. With her cool Nordic beauty, obviously a throwback to her English mother's Norse ancestors, she looked like an ice princess. An ice princess right before the thaw, he smiled to himself as he bounded up the concrete stairs that led to the imposing front entrance to her home.

The woman who opened the door to him, though, was anything but cool and his own body heated in appreciation at the transformation. Wrapped—there really was no other way to describe the way her dress clung to her body—in vibrant red, with her silver-blond hair drawn up into a loose twist off her neck and with her lips painted a luscious tone to match her dress, she was a far cry from the fragile, wounded female in jeans and a T-shirt he'd met in the gardens today.

He took a moment to take in the full effect of her stunning beauty. From top to toe she was the whole package—a package that sent a jolt of pure lust burning through his body.

"You look amazing," he blurted with all the finesse of a randy twelfth grader heading to senior prom.

"Thank you," she replied, her full lips pulling into a tempting curve. "You clean up pretty well yourself."

He offered her his arm. "Shall we go?"

Her fingertips seared through the fine cotton of his shirt as she rested her hand elegantly on his forearm. "Where are we going?"

He named a restaurant that clearly garnered her immediate approval.

"Very nice, I haven't been there in a while," she said with a nod of her head.

Intimate and with excellent food, Marcus knew the place was exalted by food lovers who moved in only the best social circles. There was usually a waiting list to get through its hallowed doors but he hadn't scholarshipped his way through the best prep schools and colleges in Boston without learning a thing or two about contacts. A quick call to an influential old college roommate, who now worked in the financial sector here in London, and the reservation had been a fait accompli.

Marcus handed Avery into the passenger seat of the car and as he settled himself behind the wheel she turned to speak to him.

"You okay driving on the left-hand side of the road?"

"I got here safely enough, didn't I?" he answered with a smile. "Seriously though, I come to the U.K. fairly often, you're safe with me."

Safe enough in the car perhaps, he amended silently. What happened during dinner and, hopefully after, was another thing entirely. And there it was, that intense burning need for her, rocketing through his veins—and other parts of him. Parts he fully intended to ignore, but they were not so easily disregarded. His body thrummed with awareness of her presence beside him, of the subtle floral fragrance she wore that tempted him to find out if she tasted as sweet as she smelled. Marcus's fingers tightened on the steering wheel, as he forced himself back under control. There was plenty of time to indulge in how she made him feel. For now he simply had to ensure that she'd be open to further discussion. He wasn't about to let physical desire stand in the way of garnering the most influential sale of his career.

Traffic was surprisingly light as they drove toward the restaurant. Gliding the car to a halt in front of the valet stand, Marcus quickly alighted and went around to Avery's door to help her from the vehicle, relishing the opportunity to watch her long slender legs as she swung them out of the car. Avery gracefully rose on silver spike-heeled sandals that did all kinds of wicked things to his imagination, and Marcus was struck anew by her almost ethereal beauty.

Heads turned as they were ushered in through the front door. The maître d' greeted them both by name. He shouldn't have been surprised. While his research had told him that Avery grew up every inch a privileged, although shy, sun-kissed California girl, she'd spent considerable time the past few years on the charity circuit between L.A. and here. Until her father's sudden illness, that was. After that, she'd dropped out of circulation, not reappearing in the public eye until now, months after Forrest Cullen's death. An unexpected surge of protectiveness welled up inside him as those turning heads, one by one, swiveled back to their dinner companions, the buzz of conversation suddenly rising in the rarified atmosphere of the restaurant.

Always one to take the bull by the horns, Marcus inclined his head to Avery's and whispered in her ear, "Looks like you've just become the main topic of conversation, hmm?"

She nodded, a brief jerk of her slender neck. The action seemed totally at odds with her innate poise and beauty. "Some people never did have anything better to do."

Even though she'd brushed off the reaction of the restaurant patrons, the hint of bitterness in her tone spoke volumes and he realized what an ordeal it had been for her to walk past the other tables. Her hand had tightened on his arm the moment she'd been recognized and he'd felt her relief when they were shown to their table for two, set off in an intimate alcove near the rear of the restaurant.

"From their reactions I'd say it looks like it's been a while since you've been in circulation," he said carefully after they'd been seated and provided with menus. He didn't want her to know that he'd investigated her so thoroughly.

"I haven't been out much," she said carefully. "It wasn't

as hard as I thought it would be—to drop out of circulation, I mean."

He reached a hand across the table, lightly brushing her forearm. "Thank you for coming out with me tonight."

He felt, rather than saw, her reaction to his touch. The way her skin tautened beneath his fingertips, tiny goose bumps rising as if a shiver had passed through her body. Her gaze locked with his and he saw the flare of sensual awareness that blazed deep within her eyes. Eyes that were suddenly molten, before she obviously shut down the feeling as effectively as if she'd been doused in a glacier-fed lake. Giving an internal shrug, Marcus decided not to pursue her reaction just yet. After all, it didn't take him closer to his goal and it had clearly disturbed her. He wasn't quite sure which of those reasons struck him most strongly—his need to secure the sale of the Cullen Collection, or the near overwhelming urge to further explore the burgeoning awareness that pulsed between them.

"It was nice to be asked," she said, simply fighting to maintain her composure.

Inside, however, was a different story. She was shocked at how such a simple gesture could cause such a riotous reaction. His caress had been light, impersonal even, and yet it felt as if a thousand tiny energy bolts danced under her skin. Her eyes flew up to meet his. In the subdued lighting of the restaurant they were a darker green than she remembered, more like the mesmerizing glow of a flawless emerald. She felt her internal muscles clench on a rise of intense physical interest.

Marcus Price was dangerous. Not only was he a threat to her equilibrium, he was very definitely a man on a mission. She couldn't afford to lower her guard or who knew what he might get her to agree to do.

It had been a long time since anyone had shown her attention that wasn't aimed at garnering something back for the donor. She never used to care all that much. She had a few close friends and a far wider group of acquaintances who she could rely on for a fun time. But when her father became ill, and the seriousness of his illness became apparent, she'd realized how shallow she'd allowed her life to become. And it had opened her eyes to the truth that the only person she honestly could rely on was herself—provided she remained true to herself all the time.

She'd meant what she'd said. It *was* nice to be asked. Prior to her father's illness, her group of friends had formed a habit of directing her to wherever they happened to be. Her sheltered upbringing had only served to feed her natural shyness and insecurities and she'd initially welcomed their direction. Perhaps her behavior had been born out of her own desire to be a part of something, anything—to simply belong. But they'd been using her in their own way, and she'd let them. Convincing herself she enjoyed their company, the endlessly dull nights of partying, picking up the tab at the end of the evening without so much as batting an eyelid. Oh, yes, she'd been popular all right.

A hint of bitterness lingered on her tongue at the memory. She'd been so hopelessly naive. Would Marcus be any different than the others? she wondered. Would he expect her to pick up the tab for tonight? Well, she could only wait and see. He'd stated his reasons for seeing her right from the start and despite her rather unnerving reaction to him, she knew exactly where she stood. Marcus Price was in for a surprise if he thought he could railroad her into doing *anything* she didn't want to.

He was unexpectedly good company and Avery was impressed by Marcus's astute observations on the art world. She could hear it in his voice, his enthusiasm for his profession and his determination to succeed. But there was more to his drive to move up the ranks within Waverly's—he genuinely loved and appreciated the works he handled. His appreciation for them was obvious in his every word.

Growing up as she had, she'd been surrounded by genuine art lovers as well as those who only saw art as an investment opportunity. She knew well how to tell the difference. Her father had been an intriguing combination of the two, a fact that had made him sought out by individuals, museums and galleries alike for his opinion on specific works.

Marcus seemed to have many of her dad's qualities when it came to discussing specific works. He was knowledgeable and perceptive in his remarks, but most of all—perhaps most disconcertingly—he was passionate, too. By the time they were sipping coffee and lingering over the simple dessert of mixed fresh berries and cream he'd ordered for them to share she found herself not wanting the evening to end.

Nothing like her usual escorts, he'd only had one glass of wine through dinner and, more importantly, hadn't pressed her to continue drinking when he himself had stopped. His solicitousness had come as a surprise. From the brief phone call she'd had from him last month, and the subsequent calls and emails she'd avoided, he'd struck her as being both pushy and persistent. And yet tonight he'd been anything but.

As he gestured to the waiter for their bill she found herself wishing she'd met him under different circumstances. Circumstances that didn't involve his trying to procure her father's collection. On that thought she realized she'd allowed herself to be lulled into beginning to think there was more to this evening than there could be. But, she reminded herself sternly, the Marcus Prices of this world usually operated on one agenda. She was a conduit to what he wanted. She had no illusions about that.

The waiter laid the discreet black-leather wallet containing their bill on the table between them. Avery went to reach for it, out of habit, but Marcus's hand settled heavily upon hers.

"What do you think you're doing?" he asked, an odd expression on his face that was part confusion and part injured-male pride.

"What does it look like I'm doing? I'm picking up the tab, of course."

"No, you are not," he said firmly, lifting her hand from the bill. "I can't believe you thought I'd ask you out to dinner and expect you to pay."

"I'm more than happy to split the check. It's been a lovely evening."

"Avery, I asked you as my guest. Even if I hadn't, I still wouldn't expect you to pay for anything."

He slotted his credit card inside the wallet and nodded as the waiter returned to lift it from the table.

"Ah, yes," she said, "this is a business expense for you, after all."

He shot her another look, and this time there was no mistaking the irritation on his face. "Is that what you think?"

"Well, isn't it?" she challenged.

He sat back in his chair, his eyes never leaving her face. He gave a short, sharp nod. "It might have started that way," he conceded.

Avery felt a surge of hope swell inside her. Started that way? So where did that leave them now? Was he as attracted to her as she was to him? The waiter returned, preventing Marcus from saying anything further and she watched as he signed his name on the chit with a flourish, adding a tip in cash at the same time.

"Come on," he said, rising from the table. "I think we should go."

She'd offended him, she just knew it. Aside from placing his hand possessively at the small of her back as they left the restaurant and waited for the valet to bring his car around, he said nothing. He saw her settled into the soft leather of her seat before again taking the wheel and driving back toward her home. When he pulled up outside the front entrance she quickly unbuckled her seat belt and turned to face him.

"Marcus, I'm sorry," she said. "I didn't mean to offend you."

He looked steadily back at her and she saw the exact moment the irritation he'd been bristling with left him. He raised one hand to her cheek, his fingertips a featherlight touch on her skin. A touch that left her wanting more, wanting him.

"No, it's my fault," he said. "You were right. I did have an ulterior motive when I suggested we go out together. I didn't expect it to change into something else, that's all."

"S-something else?" she asked.

"Yeah," he said, leaning forward to close the distance between them. "This."

The hand that had been touching her cheek slid around to cup the back of her neck before his lips gently descended. The instant his mouth touched hers she gasped a soft sound of surrender. His kiss was sweet, almost over before it had begun but it was enough to leave her senses reeling, her breath uneven in a chest that suddenly felt constricted.

"I want to see you again, Avery," he whispered, resting his forehead against hers, his warm hand still cupping the back of her head, his fingers gently massaging her sensitized skin.

Everything inside her screamed *yes!* But caution urged her to refuse him. She'd sworn she wouldn't allow herself to be used again, to be surrounded by fair-weather friends who only wanted whatever she could provide without giving anything, not even loyalty, in return. She thought carefully about how Marcus had been at dinner. Entertaining, solicitous, kind, even. Pushy? No. Nor did he badger her about the collection. Maybe he was different than the others. Maybe he genuinely wanted *her*. Hopefully about as much as she wanted him—as much as she had, in all honesty, since the first time she laid eyes on him. There was only one way she'd find out. Was she prepared to take that risk?

Avery drew in a shaky breath before replying. "I'd like that. Tomorrow?"

"Sure, tomorrow it is. I have some gallery visits scheduled for the morning but how about I stop by after lunch?"

"Perfect. I'll be here."

He waited in the car as she ascended the stairs and let herself in the front door, waving back briefly in response to her salute as she stood illuminated by the overhead light. And as he started the car and headed back down the driveway, Avery wondered whether she'd done the right thing. Was she setting herself up for failure? Or could he turn out to be the best thing that had happened to her in a very, very long time?

Four

Sleep remained elusive all night long and by the time the sun began to show its face, in all its golden splendor, Avery was relieved to be able to push back her tumbled sheets and head for the pool downstairs. A set of punishing laps would clear her head, and maybe go some way to ridding her body of the nervous tension that held her in its grip.

What had she been thinking last night? She'd had one glass of wine—one!—and yet she'd been putty in his hands. Worse, she had *wanted* to be putty in his hands.

Avery slipped on a jewel-blue one-piece suit and raced down the stairs to the basement lap pool her father had had installed several years ago. She dove immediately into the water and powered straight to the end, flipping neatly and heading back the way she'd come. Again and again, end over end, until her muscles were screaming for surcease. Even then, she pushed herself another four laps before dragging herself from the water and lying on the tiled edge, her chest heaving with the need for more oxygen. Eventually her body calmed, but her mind was not as acquiescent. She still couldn't get Marcus Price out of her thoughts, and with those thoughts came that tension all over again.

She grabbed a towel and wrapped it around her before heading back to her room to shower and change. Once dressed in her habitual jeans and a clean T-shirt, she went to her studio and gathered her things. The day had dawned bright and clear and she was determined to make the most of the light that Marcus had pointed out was so lacking in her painting. Never one for breakfast, she knew Mrs. Jackson would bring out fresh coffee and a muffin or scone to her later in the morning and she wanted to get a good start before then.

After yesterday's gloom and cloud, today's sunshine was a delightful contrast and the warmth filled her with a new vigor. The new gardener was busy already, thinning out the spent roses, and Avery could already see the progress he'd made on the weeds that tenaciously asserted their presence. Seeing her father's favorite garden being restored to its former glory filled her with happiness although, even here, he hadn't allowed Avery too close.

She didn't remember her mother ever working out here—she'd died when Avery was only five. But her father had told her of her mother's joy in planning the garden, how hands-on she'd been in its planting, how closely she'd supervised the garden staff to ensure her precious plants received the care she knew they deserved. Those memories had driven him out here again and again, striving perhaps to rediscover the closeness he'd shared with his dead wife for far too short a time.

Avery's favorite memories of this garden had included a small but perfect marble-angel statue—one to which she'd poured her child's heart out to as her mother grew less and less accessible. Diagnosed with cancer during her pregnancy with Avery, Sybil Cullen had eschewed treatment until her baby girl had been born, only then embracing all that the medical professionals could offer her. It had given her five years with her treasured daughter and Avery had always associated the statue with her mother. She'd been devastated to come to the garden a few weeks after her mother's funeral to find the statue gone.

Apparently, deeply depressed after his wife's death, Forrest Cullen had found its presence to be an angelic reminder of his own personal tragedy and that nothing ever remained the same. He'd sold it with no compunction. On finding his daughter desolately sobbing in the garden when she should have been safely tucked up in bed, he had been shaken to learn just how fond of the statue Avery had been. He'd done his best to buy it back but had eventually given up as it appeared to have disappeared from the art world without a trace. Avery had recently set up a message board on the internet to try to discover the statue. She was prepared to pay just about anything to get it back where it belonged.

Strangely enough that had been how she'd met her new gardener—through the forum, created specifically for tracing art and antiquities, where she'd established her message board. When he'd first made contact with her, he'd apparently been working on a ranch back in the States. It was only after she'd posted photos of the garden from her mother's time, and then from today, that he'd mentioned he was planning to travel to London and offered a few weeks of his time to help her get the garden back in order.

Frustrated by her own lack of progress in the garden, Avery had gone out on a limb and hired him as a casual gardener without checking references or credentials or anything. From what she could tell so far, his only fault was the fact he was a bit of a drifter, but then establishing a home and hearth wasn't for everyone. Being a homebody herself, she couldn't imagine a life like his. She shook her head and wondered how strange it would feel to come from all that glorious space on a ranch to something as enclosed as a Kensington garden.

Either way, she was grateful he'd made the transition. He'd already made great inroads.

She set up her easel and set to work, humming a tune while she did so.

"You sound happy," a deep male voice drawled from the shrubbery. "Always good to hear."

Avery watched as her newest employee straightened from beneath the foliage and rose to his full height. Astonishing clear blue eyes met hers out from under a thoroughly disreputable hat that should probably have been confiscated by border control. He looked to be in his sixties and his rangy, fit build spoke of a man who'd done some hard physical labor in his time.

He wiped one hand on a pair of well-worn denims and tipped his hat to her.

"Good morning, Miss Cullen. She's a beauty, isn't she?"

"Good morning to you, too, Mr. Wells. It looks as if it will be a lovely day. I see you've been busy already."

"Please, call me Ted," he corrected her with a smile that made her suddenly think of silver-screen stars from the fifties. Persuasive, perfectly handsome, yet with that edge of devil-may-care lurking about the edges. "So," he said, rocking back on his heels, "are you always this happy when you work?"

She felt the uncomfortable heat of a blush stain her cheeks. It really was none of his business but for some reason she felt compelled to confide in him. Goodness knew she didn't really have anyone else. She didn't want to impose on Macy, who was busy planning her wedding and, with renovations on the inn she'd converted into a drama school complete, she was now looking at opening the school. Macy's days were busy enough without being worried by what might or might not happen between Avery and Marcus. Avery's only other potential confidante, Mrs. Jackson, was so protective of her she was just as likely to scold Avery for even thinking of spending time with Marcus, and she definitely wasn't in the mood for that.

From their first meeting online in the art forum and during their subsequent discussions over the past couple of months, and then in person a few days ago when he'd arrived for his first day of work, he'd struck her as the type of guy who'd hold a confidence close to his chest.

"I've met someone," she said, almost shyly. "I don't really know if it'll go anywhere."

"What's he like? Do you trust him?"

She shrugged. "Good question. I barely know him except for the fact he's tenacious."

"That can be a good thing."

"And a bad one, too. He wants to represent my father's art collection at sale, and he won't listen when I say it's definitely not for sale."

"You have your father's collection here?" Ted asked, tilting his hat back a bit off his forehead.

"No, it's back in L.A."

"Any particular reason you don't want to sell it? Don't you think he'll do a good enough job?"

Avery pressed her lips together before answering. Why did everyone think she should just let the collection go? Didn't they understand what it had meant to her dad?

"He's with Waverly's. I don't doubt they'd do a very professional job, but as to my reason for not wanting to sell, it's personal," she answered, not bothering to hide the note of irritation that tainted her words.

Ted Wells cracked a half smile and nodded. "Personal is good enough. I've heard of Waverly's, they seem to know their stuff. You know, if this guy is with them, maybe you should ask him to help you track down that statue you've been looking for. With his contacts he might be able to succeed where you've struggled to find information in the past.

Plus, if he's willing to help you, it might show whether his character is true."

Avery considered his words. As old-fashioned as the term *character* was, Ted very well might be right. She suddenly felt churlish for sounding so annoyed just a moment ago.

"Look, I'm sorry if I sounded rude."

"No problem, you don't want to let the collection go. That's fine."

"Sometimes I feel like it's all I have left of my father, y'know? He loved it so much," she found herself blurting out.

Compassion filled the older man's eyes. "You think he didn't love you as much?"

His words pulled no punches, they forced Avery to search deep into her heart for the truth. Sure, there'd been times when she'd felt unloved, what child didn't at one stage or another? Perhaps her father hadn't been as demonstrative as she would have liked, perhaps he'd been distant but he'd still been her father. Deep down, she knew he had loved her.

Ted bent to clear a section of weeds that poked through a herbaceous border and continued talking without waiting for her reply. "Paintings are only things. I'm pretty sure that your dad's love for you was more than just a thing. I was never lucky enough to have kids, but I'd hope that if I had they'd know that no matter what, my love was something they could hold in their hearts and minds forever. Love's like that, y'know?"

There was more than a grain of truth in what Ted said.

"So you think I should let them go?"

Ted shrugged and reached for the shears hanging on his belt loop, taking his time to snip a couple of dead stems off a nearby hydrangea. "That's not for me to say. From what you've told me before, I'd hazard a guess that your father'd be sorry if he knew the paintings weren't able to be appreciated by people who'd enjoy them like he had."

There was something soothing in the measured way Ted

spoke. Even though they'd only met online before today, and shared the briefest of phone calls establishing when he could start work in the garden, she felt as if he'd been around for a whole lot longer.

Avery sighed. "You're probably right. I just don't know if I'm ready."

Ted nodded. "You'll know when, or even if, it's the right time. They say Waverly's is supposed to be one of the best so, if you do decide to sell, the collection will be in the right hands when the time comes. In the meantime, think about getting that young man of yours to find the angel for you."

"Oh, he's not my young man," she protested. *Not yet, anyway,* a tiny voice whispered inside her mind. "But I'll think about your suggestion. Thanks."

"Anytime," he said, gathering up the weeds and cuttings and loading them into a wheelbarrow. "If you need me I'll be working around the front of the house for a few hours."

When he was gone, Avery turned to her painting, giving it her most critical eye. Marcus had been one hundred percent right about what was wrong with it. Not to mention his observation that her heart wasn't fully invested in the rendition of the garden. She let her gaze wander to the spot where the angel statue had once stood, seeing it as clearly in her mind's eye as if it hadn't been gone for the past nineteen years. The soft, almost fleshlike tones of the marble, the graceful sweep of the angel's wings, the way the arms had curved gently in the air as if plucking some precious unseen thing from the sky.

Without thought she reached for her palette and her paintbrushes, hooking them both deftly with her thumb as with her other hand she squeezed tubes of paint onto the scarred and paint-stained wooden surface of her palette. Time lost all meaning as she started to paint, putting back what should never have been lost all those years ago. Vaguely she was aware of Mrs. Jackson's call that her morning tea was on the terrace, but she continued to work, oblivious to time and the gnawing ache that started to grow in her stomach.

Marcus strolled along the path toward the garden where the housekeeper had told him Avery had been painting all morning. He sensed he'd made an ally when, after hearing her muttered comment about Avery not eating yet today, he'd said he'd make sure she came in for lunch.

Bees buzzed from bloom to bloom along the path, collecting the last of the pollen. Marcus had never really stopped to consider the seasons before. His life in New York was busy, sometimes even frenetic, and the change of seasons was, for him, marked by how heavy his coat was and how disrupted, or not, traffic was by snow. Stepping into this garden made him more aware of time passing, of how some things such as the spent annual plantings were at their end and of how other plants would continue on, forever green no matter the season.

It was philosophical thought of the type he didn't usually indulge in, but with it came the strong reminder that nothing remained the same—ever. If life could be defined by seasons, his grandfather was well into his autumnal years. Which didn't leave Marcus a great deal of time to restore *Lovely Woman* to where it belonged.

He'd been honest with Avery last night when he'd said that he'd started the evening with a specific motive but that motive had faded into obscurity when he found himself purely enjoying her company. But he couldn't afford to be so distracted, not again.

Avery paused in her work as he drew near and, still unaware of his approach, stepped back to gain a fresh perspective on what she was doing. He could see she'd been busy on the painting, and her skill was apparent in the improvements he could see even from this distance.

"That's looking great," he commented as he drew alongside her.

She turned to him with a happy smile on her face. "It just feels right now. Thanks for your suggestions yesterday."

"I don't remember suggesting this," he said, pointing to the angel statue that now formed the focal point of the canvas. "It's not a part of the garden, but it seems to belong here in the picture."

"That's the point." She sighed. "It *does* belong there."

Her face took on a melancholy expression that saw his protective instincts rise firmly to the fore again. "It makes you sad—why?"

"The angel statue was a wedding gift to my parents from my mother's family. I don't know exactly how old the statue was, or where it came from originally. My father sold it after my mother died. Too many painful memories for him, I guess. I was five then, and I got really upset when I realized it was gone."

"Unusual for a five-year-old to get so upset about a statue," Marcus commented, struck by her sudden vulnerability.

She shrugged. "I suppose I was a bit unusual. I know I was a lonely child, except when I was out here, in the garden, with my imagination. My mother was ill for most of the time I knew her and in the six months before she died I was pretty much left to my own devices."

His indignation must have shown on his face because she hastened to elaborate.

"Don't get me wrong. There were plenty of staff assigned to my care. I had a nanny, and Mrs. Jackson was already the housekeeper here back then and she used to look out for me all the time."

"What about your father?"

"He spent as much time as he could with my mother. They were devoted to each other."

Marcus turned away. He found it a stretch of the imagination that a couple could be so devoted to one another that they neglected their only child. It was no better than his own parents, who'd been so selfish and enslaved by drugs, needing his grandfather to take care of him. Either way, it wasn't right.

"You spent a lot of time in the garden?" he forced himself to ask.

Avery nodded, a nostalgic smile on her face. "It was my wonderland. I could hide with my coloring pencils and my paper under the tree over there, and when I needed to talk to someone, the angel was always there to listen."

Suddenly he understood why she had been so distraught when the statue had been taken away. She was an only child and, obviously, a very solitary one. It had been her friend.

"What happened to it?"

"Dad put it in the hands of his broker who found a buyer for it straightaway. By the time he found out how upset I was about it being gone, it had already changed hands again, and the seller didn't have the contact details for whomever purchased it. I have no idea where it is now, or even if it still exists."

She put her palette and brushes down then stretched her neck and rotated her shoulders, as if working out the kinks. His hands itched to reach out and massage them for her, to ease the taut muscles and replace her tension with something else. He fisted his hands and pushed them into his trouser pockets.

"Have you looked for it?"

"Oh, yes." She nodded vigorously. "Dad kept the bills of sale for everything that he bought or sold over the years, together with full descriptions of each item—it makes up quite a history when you go through them all. But even with copies of the identifying marks and old photos, I haven't been able to find a trace of it. I even set up message boards on several art and antiquities sites asking for help, but no luck." She laughed. "Oh, except in finding a new gardener!"

"Gardener?"

"Long story," she said with a wave of her hand. "I was talking with him about the statue this morning. And you."

"Me?"

"Yeah, Ted thought you might be able to use your contacts to help me find the statue. I'd be willing to pay anything to get it back."

Marcus let out a sharp bark of laughter. "Rule one in negotiations, Avery. Don't ever admit what you're prepared to pay."

A sweet stain of color lit her cheeks and she rolled her eyes. "I know that, Marcus. I'm not likely to say that to a prospective seller." All of a sudden her face grew serious. "But will you do it? Will you help me find my angel?"

It took all of about three seconds for Marcus to reach his decision. He wanted her to owe him. Big-time. If she felt she owed him, if she trusted him enough, she'd release her father's art collection. Then he could buy back *Lovely Woman*. He could just imagine his grandfather's face when he put it back on the empty hook on his living-room wall. Marcus's own private acknowledgment and heartfelt thanks for all the old man had sacrificed for him. One way or another, he was prepared to do whatever it took for however long it took. And, given how attracted he was to Avery Cullen, he looked forward to spending that time with her.

"Of course I'll help you," he said, taking her hands in his. "It's the least I can do."

And as her eyes began to shimmer with joy and relief, he forced back the conscience that told him he was nothing more than a heartless, ruthless bastard.

"You will? Really? Oh, you have no idea how grateful I am," she gushed, tears spilling from her lower lids and tracking down her cheeks.

He wiped the moisture away with the pad of his thumb, telling himself that the end, in this case, totally justified the means. She'd have her precious statue back, somehow. And his family would get back what was rightfully theirs.

Five

"When can you start?" Avery asked, her heart beating double-time in excitement. She hadn't expected Marcus to agree so readily to her request.

He gave an easy laugh that made something twinge deep inside her. She loved the way his whole face lit up when he smiled, but when he laughed it sent something tingling all the way to her toes.

"How about now?"

"Seriously? You have the time?" Avery couldn't believe her ears.

"Sure, although if your father initiated an investigation soon after he sold it and didn't come up with anything, I don't know whether I'll be successful."

"I know," Avery answered, feeling the edge of her excitement dull a little. "But maybe you can turn up something new?"

Even she could hear the desperation in her voice.

"I'll do what I can, Avery. Why don't you come in and have

some lunch before Mrs. Jackson skins us both, and then you can show me your father's records on the angel."

"I can show you straight to his study. He kept everything there, with duplicates at our L.A. home. I wonder—"

"Avery," he said, interrupting her enthusiasm. "I promised Mrs. Jackson I'd make sure you had something to eat. She tells me you haven't had anything all day."

"I don't need—" Her stomach chose to grumble loudly at that exact point, making her laugh. "Okay, maybe I do need to have some lunch."

"You think?" he said with a quizzical look on his face that rapidly dissolved into another of those killer smiles. He offered her his arm. "Come on, then, before Mrs. Jackson takes a contract out on me for not looking after her chick."

Avery laughed and slid her hand into the crook of his arm. It was nice to know someone outside of her employment cared enough to follow up on her, even if this particular someone had already openly stated his wish to change her mind about selling her father's collection. After they'd eaten in the kitchen under the censorious gaze of the indubitable Mrs. Jackson, Avery showed Marcus into her father's study.

Even though the room had been aired regularly, she liked to think it still held a hint of her father's favorite cigars combined with the unmistakable whiff of the old papers and books that he'd accumulated over the years and added to the generations of papers already resident. She leaned across the desk and turned on the computer, before opening a file drawer and extracting a folder crammed with paper.

"Here, this is all I could find," she said, passing it to Marcus and gesturing for him to sit behind the desk in her father's antique swivel chair. Once the computer had booted up she opened the discussion forums she'd posted on during her search. "And here are the message boards."

"You've been busy," Marcus commented, flicking through

the printed information she'd given him. "And you say you haven't been able to make any headway?"

"Nothing," she admitted. "It's been really frustrating. For a while there I thought I'd tracked her to a private collector near Lake Como but while he had another piece by the same sculptor, he didn't have my angel."

"Do you have electronic versions of this information?" he asked, waving his hand over the folder.

"Most of it. Certainly of the markings and details of the sculpture."

She leaned over him to reach for the computer mouse and as she did so her breast brushed against his arm. It was as if a shock wave shot through her. A shock wave that made her skin sensitive, her breasts feel swollen and heavy, her nipples tight and begging for…something, anything, *him*. She shifted slightly, breaking the contact but it did little to lessen the desire that had caught her in its grip. Her fingers trembled as she grabbed the mouse and flicked open the file that held the data she referred to. Once she had it open, she stepped aside, keeping a good twelve inches between them as she explained the various diagrams he had begun to scroll through.

Thankfully, her voice remained steady, but that was where her equilibrium began and ended. What on earth was it about him that made her so responsive to even the slightest touch? She wasn't some shrinking virgin, although she lacked the experience of many of her peers. She'd been around attractive men before, but she'd never felt as out of control as she felt right now.

Marcus's voice dragged her concentration back to their quest. "Do you mind if I transfer these files onto a flash drive so I can work through them back at the hotel? My laptop is linked to the Waverly's server and I can probably better process some of the data that way and see if I can't explore some of these dead-end trails a bit further."

Avery chewed her lip thinking for a minute before giving

in to her instincts. She may live to regret it, but the words spilled from her mouth before she could consider them a moment longer.

"Why don't you bring your computer here? In fact, why don't you let your hotel room go and just stay here? I mean, I don't know how long you're planning to stay in England but, seriously, I have more rooms than I can use and I'd welcome the company. You are helping me after all."

He hesitated before answering, and Avery felt about as gauche as a schoolgirl meeting her crush face-to-face for the first time. She'd been ridiculously overeager. After all, hadn't she just been trying to avoid the guy for the past several months? Now she was inviting him to come and stay in her home?

"Sure," he said, and her heart gave a crazy little skip in her chest at the simplicity of his answer.

"You will?"

He looked at her and she found herself captured by his stare. "Yeah," he answered, smiling. "I will. I have appointments I'll need to attend but I have some time off owed to me, as well. I don't see why I can't take it here. Let me clear it with the office but in the meantime, I can move my things here tomorrow morning if that suits you?"

If it suited her? She filled with a combination of delight and anxiety. Oh, it suited her all right. And if he could help her recover the angel statue, it would suit her a whole lot more.

Marcus checked out of his hotel after breakfast and tossed his suit carrier in the trunk of the Jag. He'd only expected to be in London a few days, but if he was going to stay here a little longer he'd probably need to add to his wardrobe. He was all clear to stay for a couple of weeks, though, on condition he did a very specific job for Ann Richardson, the CEO of Waverly's. She'd been cagey about why she hadn't asked anyone actually working in-house to do the research she'd requested, and she'd asked Marcus to forward his findings direct to her personal email.

With that charter in mind he knew this represented another opportunity to shine. Ann was the kind of boss who encouraged growth in her staff and rewarded it in kind. And he knew just the level of reward he wanted. It was his goal to be Waverly's youngest partner and this opening, hopefully coupled with securing the Cullen Collection for representation, would see him realize his dream before his approaching twenty-eighth birthday.

Ann's request had intrigued him on several levels but mostly because she wanted it done on the quiet—making the most of the fact that he wasn't working from his New York office. Waverly's rogue collector, Roark Black, had gone to Dubai to procure a collection that included treasures that would incite the avarice of even the most parsimonious sultan. One piece in particular, an ancient statue inlaid with pure gold, was expected to bring in upward of two hundred million dollars and it was this item that Ann had asked him to research further.

The publicity surrounding the auction was anticipated to be huge and Waverly's reputation, not to mention Ann's, was on the line. If the statue turned out to be stolen, as an unsubstantiated rumor currently circulating had suggested, the fallout would be irreparably damaging. It had also been suggested that perhaps Roark Black's methods hadn't been entirely aboveboard in securing the piece for auction, and, by association, Ann Richardson was being tarred with the same brush. While his track record on finding treasures was impeccable, and he'd personally authenticated the piece that was the jewel in the crown of the upcoming auction, Black himself had dropped off the radar and was unavailable for further comment. But Ann trusted the man, and that was enough for Marcus.

He smiled to himself as he negotiated the route toward

Avery's home in Kensington. It was a good thing research was one of his strong points because between the two statues, the Gold Heart and the angel, he had a whole lot of work ahead of him.

"Are you sure it's okay that I help you with researching the Gold Heart statues?" Avery asked later that evening as they settled in her father's study after dinner.

"I checked with Ann and explained the resources you have here in your library, and she okayed it," Marcus said. He himself had been surprised that Ann had approved his request for an assistant and his suggestion that it be Avery Cullen had met with a moment's silence before Ann had agreed on condition he could trust Avery implicitly to keep any information confidential. "Besides, who knows your father's system better than you? Right? We're lucky he has such an extensive collection of reference materials. We may as well make the most of the resources available to us."

Avery nodded carefully but he could still see the faint lines of worry on her face. Could she sense his urgency, his relief that they could conduct this research without taking it into the public domain?

"It's okay," he reiterated, as much for himself as for her.

"But what if I'm useless at this?"

For all her money and poise she lacked even the most fundamental level of self-confidence. It was a combination that spoke to his basest male instincts and was intensely appealing.

"Seriously," she insisted. "I do charity work and I dabble in painting. I'm no research assistant."

"Don't sell yourself short," he answered firmly. "You are a great deal more than a dabbler and even I've heard about what you've achieved through your charity work. You're exactly what I need."

He let the double entendre hang on the air between them, noting the instant his words struck home in all their contexts.

"Well," she said, drawing in a swift breath, "when you put it that way, how can I refuse?"

He settled into the chair behind the desk while Avery thoughtfully perused her father's card catalog for anything on the Gold Heart statues. He'd been meticulous in his cross-referencing and before long she'd pulled a stack of books from the shelves and, curling up on the padded corner window seat, began to flick through them while Marcus scanned international internet sites for any recent articles. They worked in relative silence for nearly an hour before a soft sound from her dragged his attention from the computer screen.

"What is it?" he asked. "Did you find something?"

Avery shifted so she was sitting upright and paged through the book in her lap until she found the right spot. "Well, there's an awful lot of data about the statues and what they look like, when they were created and all that. But did you know the legend attached to them?"

Marcus got up from his chair and sat next to her on the window seat. As he did so, her soft sweet fragrance wafted around him. Right now, as interested as he was in what she'd found out about the statues, all he wanted to do was bury his face in her hair and inhale the goodness of her.

"Tell me," he said, forcing his hands to remain at his sides when his every instinct begged him to reach out and touch her. To trail his fingers through her silky white-blond hair. To taste her lips and see if they were as enticing as they'd been on Saturday night when their date had ended and he'd had to be content with a chaste kiss good-night.

"This book has the most information on the Gold Heart statues of Rayas. It says here that three statues were originally commissioned by the country's ruler. They sound exquisite. Look, here's a photo of one of them."

She turned the book to face him, leaning in to him a little as she did so. It seemed only natural to put his nearest arm behind her. She fit just under his shoulder—perfectly so. Too perfectly. Marcus forced his concentration on the page before them. The photo, while in color, probably didn't do the statue justice.

Standing on a plinth of inch-thick gold, and boasting a pure golden heart inlaid on its breast, the two-foot-high figure of a woman was breathtaking.

"Do you think it was modeled on a real woman?" Avery asked.

"She was very beautiful, if it was. Although probably a bit short for my tastes," he teased.

Avery elbowed him in his side. "Oh, stop it, you're being disrespectful. I thought you had to take this seriously."

Even though she scolded him, he could see the reluctant smile pulling at her enticing lips. And she was right. All joking aside, this was very serious. Ann had been contacted by a sheikh from Rayas accusing her of selling stolen property—specifically, *his* stolen property. If the statue Roark Black had procured was stolen, it cast everyone associated with it in a very bad light. Loss of industry respect and clientele notwithstanding, the legal ramifications were damning. Waverly's would go down, and, as captain of the ship, Ann Richardson would be totally sunk with it.

"Okay, I apologize. Tell me more," he coaxed.

"The statues were originally commissioned for the king's three daughters to bring them luck in love for as long as the statues graced the palaces they lived in. According to the legend the daughters *were* lucky in love, as were several generations after them. It seems that a century ago, one of the statues went missing—some say it went down with the *Titanic* but I can't find anything to substantiate that. Correspondingly, that particular branch of the family met with ill health and bad luck—in both love and money. They say there isn't a surviving member of that branch of the family still living today. Isn't that just so terribly sad?"

"Tough to think your life hangs on the balance of whether

you have a statue," Marcus said, suddenly struck by Avery's deep-seated need to recover her angel statue.

Did she somehow think the carved block of marble was somehow linked to her own happiness and well-being? Surely not. But he knew exactly what it meant to lose a family heirloom, and how that loss remained a gaping hole in a family's life afterward. Maybe the old legend extended beyond Rayas's sandy borders.

Six

When Marcus woke early the next morning, it was still mostly dark outside although the hint of dawn could be seen streaking long apricot-tinged fingers through the clouds he spied through his open bedroom window. Getting to sleep last night had been near impossible—the difficulty born of dual frustrations. One, that Avery Cullen slept, alone, about three doors down the same corridor along which he'd been shown last night.

The other was that, despite him and Avery spending two more hours scouring for further information, all they'd found was one dead end after another.

When they'd decided to call it a night, Marcus had made a quick call to Ann, who'd suggested that he attempt to speak directly with Prince Raif, the Rayas prince who'd accused her of dealing in stolen antiquities. If anyone might possibly have the answers it should be the prince, although Marcus doubted that his reception would be warm, if the guy even agreed to speak with him.

He'd booked a call to His Royal Highness, Prince Raif of Rayas, for this morning, after a quick check online had confirmed Rayas was only three hours ahead of London, which meant it was nearing 9:00 a.m. there now. He had time for a quick shower and then he would make the call.

A few minutes later he was back in the study and dialing the number Ann had given him last night. It took a while, and being passed through various escalating levels of staff, but eventually the clear clipped tones of Prince Raif greeted him.

"Good morning, Your Highness. Thank you for agreeing to speak with me."

"No thank you is necessary, Mr. Price. Though I'm sure you can appreciate, Waverly's is not my favorite topic of conversation these days."

The man's crisp enunciation spoke of his higher education having been conducted abroad, possibly even here in the United Kingdom. Even so, his voice still carried the slight lilt specific to his country.

"I can understand that, however I believe your accusations are unfounded. I'm conducting research into them now and—"

"Unfounded? I think not. My family's Gold Heart statue was stolen. Several months later, your firm miraculously secures a Gold Heart and is preparing to hawk it for sale. That certainly stretches the credibility of coincidence, wouldn't you agree? Let me make one thing perfectly clear, I am not impressed with your employer's ethics."

As a shutdown, the prince's response was pretty effective, yet Marcus was not one to be deterred easily.

"It's not outside of the realm of possibility that the statue catalogued in our inventory could be the one that went missing a century ago, is it?" he insisted.

The prince sighed, the sound weighted with irritation. "Yes, Mr. Price, it is. That statue was irrevocably lost. You should expect to hear from both the FBI and Interpol, who are looking into the matter now. I suggest you encourage your Ms. Richardson to either take the necessary steps to return what rightfully belongs to my family, or to admit the item in her possession is a fake."

"And if it isn't a fake?" Marcus asked, wishing like mad that Ann had been able to track Roark Black down and get the information they so sorely needed directly from him. Even if they could just see the statue, it would help. But, ever mindful of security, Black had secured it in his private vault at an undisclosed overseas location before disappearing into the Amazon, leaving only photographs and his own authentication for Ann's records.

The prince interrupted his thoughts. "If the statue in Waverly's possession is not a fake, then one way or another you are dealing in stolen property. Specifically *my* property."

"What of the legend, Your Highness? Do you believe that for as long as a Gold Heart statue resides in a royal palace in Rayas that the family within it will always be lucky in love?"

He heard Prince Raif's sharply indrawn breath. When the man spoke it was with a barely leashed temper. "That is my family's business alone, and has no bearing on the theft."

"I didn't mean to offend you, but I would like to understand a little more about the statues and their meaning for your family."

There was a brief silence at the end of the line before the prince spoke again. This time there was a different note to his voice. "Let me say this, the absence of the statue has caused pain to my family. Do you have any brothers or sisters, Mr. Price?"

"No, I don't," Marcus admitted.

The information Avery had uncovered regarding the curse of the Gold Heart statues tickled the back of Marcus's mind. Had something happened to Prince Raif, or even the younger sister he kept so sheltered from the prying eyes of the public and international media? Was that responsible for the change in his tone? Perhaps his was a personal pain, rather than one borne on behalf of family.

"Then you can't possibly begin to understand the depths of my concern. Tell your Ms. Richardson that if she wishes to discuss this matter any further I expect her to do so face-to-face, and not to hide behind her staff."

Before Marcus could respond, the prince had severed their connection. Putting his cell phone on the desk in front of him Marcus accepted he was at a stalemate. He opened his laptop and swiftly composed a message to Ann's private email, detailing the conversation he'd just had with Prince Raif and putting in writing the sparse information he'd given her by phone the night before. None of it would make her happy.

Once he'd fired the email off he closed the lid on his laptop and leaned back in the leather swivel chair, raising his hands behind his head and expelling a breath in frustration.

"Is everything okay, Marcus?"

Avery stood in the doorway wearing a sleek black one-piece swimsuit beneath an untied robe. Every nerve in his body went on high alert at the sight of her long legs, slender figure and lightly tanned skin. The suit, while respectfully covering a great deal of her, still revealed the shape and fullness of her breasts, the curve of her tiny waist and the slight flare of her hips. All thoughts of statues fled his mind as he was faced with the beauty of the flesh-and-blood woman in the doorway.

"Marcus?" she asked again as he failed to respond. Verbally, at least, he thought with a wry grimace.

"I'm fine. I just got off the phone with Prince Raif of Rayas. We're no further forward. He firmly believes the Gold Heart statue that Ann has in the auction is his family's and if it's not, then it's a fake. I can't understand it, Roark Black wouldn't make a mistake like that."

"Then maybe it's the statue that went missing a hundred years ago."

"I sure hope it is," Marcus agreed.

"Why don't you come and have a swim with me, it might help work out some of that frustration you're carrying. We've got a changing room filled with spare swimsuits if you don't have one upstairs."

Marcus thought about it for all of a second, although he doubted going for a swim with Avery would release an ounce of the tension that held his body in its grip. "I'd like that."

He followed her down the stairs and wondered whether the pool would be heated. Well, if it wasn't, it certainly would be once he hit the water.

"You can change through there," Avery said, pointing to a niche in the painted block wall.

"Thanks," he said, making his way quickly into the changing room as she slid her robe from her shoulders and dove neatly into the pool.

He shed his clothes with an indecent amount of haste and dragged on a pair of swimming trunks he'd grabbed from the shelf, grateful to see they were a bit on the full side, which would accommodate the semi-arousal he had been fighting from the second he'd seen her in the doorway.

Avery was treading water at the deepest end of the pool when Marcus came out of the changing room. Her concentration slipped for a moment, almost making her dunk herself, as she took in the perfect symmetry of his lightly muscled physique. Maybe asking him to swim with her hadn't been such a great idea after all.

Her breath caught in her throat as he dived deep into the water, swimming below the surface for the full length of the pool before surfacing in front of her.

"You finished already?" he said with that signature smile that never failed to melt her insides.

"No, just waiting for you."

"You want to race?"

"Sure," she said, "why not? Ten laps?"

He nodded. "You want me to give you a head start?"

She snorted in derision. "A head start? What do you take me for?"

"A girl," he teased. "Besides, to give you fair warning, I was ranked second on my college swim team."

"Only second," she answered in kind. "I was first."

With that she shoved off the end of the pool and began to stroke for the other end. She was ahead at the first three turns, but not by much and she had to reach deep for the energy to maintain her lead after the fifth. But, Marcus, it seemed, had been pacing her, because on the final lap he powered ahead touching the end and then turning to wait for her as she glided to the finish line.

Her lungs were burning and her arms and legs felt like jelly. She was an accomplished swimmer and laps had a boring monotony about them that she usually completed without any issue. But this had been different. She'd pushed herself to go faster than she ever did simply for fitness. And Marcus, damn him, wasn't even breathing hard.

"That must have been some swim team you were on," she commented as she got her breath back.

"Unbeaten for five years."

He reached for her, pulling her against him and treading water for them both. "I think I deserve a prize for winning, don't you?"

Her body thrilled at his touch, and as their lower bodies brushed against one another she felt the unmistakable heaviness of his erection.

"A p-prize?" she managed, dragging her attention back to his suggestion. "What kind of prize?"

"This," he said, drawing her a little closer and capturing her lips with his.

Avery's fingers clutched tight at his shoulders as she held on for dear life. But it wasn't drowning she was most afraid of—unless you counted drowning in sensation as his lips stroked across hers in a gentle caress, a caress she wanted to deepen and explore more fully. Ever since their good-night kiss last Saturday she'd wanted to repeat the experience. Repeat it, and more. She'd never been that kind of girl, though—the type to take charge, to dominate, to lead. But right now she wanted to tell Marcus, in actions rather than words, that she wanted him. Wanted him in every way a woman could want a man.

Her legs wrapped around his hips, her center pressed against his hardened ridge, her breasts crushed against the expanse of his muscled chest. Ah, yes, now his breathing was more erratic, more labored. She opened her mouth to him, tasting him as his tongue swept inside, relishing the feel of him. Everything inside her turned molten, heated with a fire and need that all too quickly threatened to consume her. And then, almost as quickly as their kiss had begun, his hands dropped to her legs, untangling them from his body, and he withdrew a small distance from her, holding her away from him.

"What's wrong?" she asked, her body silently crying out, begging for more even as his rejection of her stung.

"Wrong? Everything about this is wrong, Avery. We've only just met. I'm here as your guest, to help you—not to seduce you. I'm sorry, I should never have let that go so far. It was out of line."

He let her go completely and she gripped the side of the pool with white-knuckled fingers.

But what if I want to be seduced? she asked deep in the recesses of her mind. But even if she'd verbalized the question he wouldn't have heard her. He'd already begun to swim, with a short choppy freestyle, to the other end of the pool, where he pulled himself from the water. She got a glimpse of his broad naked back tapering to his slim waist, his buttocks shielded by the wet black fabric of his swimming trunks, his legs long and powerful, before he grabbed a towel from the shelves and wrapped it around himself. He didn't even pause to get showered, instead grabbing his clothes from the changing room and, still wrapped in the towel, heading straight for the stairs.

With a shuddering sigh, Avery let go of the breath she'd been holding. She didn't know whether to nurse her feelings of rejection that he'd cut things short between them after setting her afire, or to be relieved he was, after all, a gentleman.

By the time she'd followed him out of the pool and showered and dressed upstairs in her room she'd managed to calm her ragged senses into some type of order. It was a matter of having to because she had no time to indulge in mentally replaying what had happened at the pool, even though her body still hummed with frustration.

Today was what she privately called a work day, which meant selecting the finer of her designer-daywear outfits and putting on a public face at a meeting of one the art charities she was involved in. This was the first time since her father's death that she'd be attending in person and it was important she be there as it was the final meeting before the upcoming weekend's major annual fund-raiser. The charity was one she was particularly passionate about as it offered children from all walks of life a chance to grow their talents.

She popped her head into the study on her way to the kitchen for cup of coffee before leaving, but Marcus wasn't there.

"Mrs. Jackson," she started as she entered the kitchen a few short minutes later, "has Mr. Price had breakfast yet?"

"No, Miss Cullen. He asked me to let you know that he'll be away from the house all day. He had some business north of London, apparently. He said he may not be back tonight and not to wait up for him."

Ah, there it was again, that stinging sense of rejection. She tried not to let it hurt, but it did nonetheless.

"I see, well, I'm sure he's a very busy man."

Mrs. Jackson gave her a searching look. "He also said to say he'd be working on the matter you asked him to look into upon his return."

A swell of hope blossomed inside. Maybe his business out of London today wasn't him running away from her after all.

"Thank you," she said with a smile on her face that felt as if it went all the way to her foolish heart.

Marcus cursed himself for every kind of fool for running away from Avery the day before. He was a man of the world. Someone quite capable of dallying with a beautiful woman, especially to get something he wanted. Somewhere along the line though, as he'd held her in his arms in the pool yesterday morning, he'd lost sight of his goals. Again. She had a way of messing with his mind that he couldn't afford to indulge. The distance created by the trip yesterday had been vitally necessary to remind himself of exactly why he'd come to England in the first place. *Lovely Woman* had to return to his family.

He'd talked to his grandfather on the phone last night and had stupidly mentioned seeing the painting. The silence that had echoed all the way from Boston had been deafening.

"The Cullens bought it back, then," his grandfather had said with a note of finality that Marcus had hated with every bone in his body. "They're not likely to let it go again, are they." It was a statement, not a question.

"I'm working on it, Grampa."

It was all he could say and the futility of the statement left him nursing a fury that was only further fed by the memory of Avery Cullen in his arms. Of the slick smooth wetness of her swimsuit beneath his hands, of the sensation of her long lean muscles moving beneath that fabric. Of the feel of her legs as they'd wrapped around his hips and the heated core of her as it settled against the aching erection he'd been forced to sustain for the greater part of the morning.

She got to him on so many levels it wasn't funny. Him, the original user. The guy who'd used his unmistakable charm to fake his way to pedigree in a way that had never seen a single fellow student question his humble blue-collar Boston background through school and subsequently through college. He was immune to the vulnerable; he'd trained himself to be. Because, to him, Marcus Price was the kind of guy who never took his eye off the prize, and he was always prepared to work hard and use his intelligence to get whatever it was that he wanted.

You want Avery Cullen, a voice snaked through the back of his mind. He acknowledged the words, accepted them, then filed them away. Sure, he wanted Avery. What heterosexual man in his right mind wouldn't want her? She was a goddess to look at, with a body that promised untold sensual delight yet she still maintained an air of sexual naiveté, of untapped raw passion, that was enough to entice even the most jaded of souls. But he wanted *Lovely Woman* more.

And it was with that avowal in the forefront of his mind that he returned to Avery's Kensington home.

He expected the atmosphere to be strained when he caught up with Avery over lunch, but she acted warm and friendly. In fact, aside from a light flush on her cheeks when they met again, she acted as if nothing had passed between them and as if his sudden departure yesterday had been nothing but normal. He hated to admit it, but it bugged him that she could be so nonchalant, and when she issued an invitation to him to attend a charity bash with her over the weekend he rapidly accepted. Held in the stately home of one of her family's old friends, it would give him more avenues to solicit contacts for future business and may well even help him in his quest to track down the angel statue that Avery was so fixated on.

On Friday afternoon, they traveled together to Fernclere Castle. Even among his influential college friends' families, Marcus had never before seen such an astounding monument to wealth and longevity as he did when they drove down the castle driveway.

"What do you think?" Avery asked, a mischievous look in her eyes.

"I think it says a lot for their business acumen that they're still private owners."

She nodded. "Yes, and they're avid collectors of fine art, too. It's part of why they agree to host this fund-raiser each year. You'll enjoy visiting the long gallery."

Marcus felt his interest lift. Potential clientele aside, there was little he enjoyed more these days than viewing privately owned collections. Inside the castle they were shown to their rooms and invited to meet with the hosts downstairs for cocktails before dinner. Avery had warned him they followed old-fashioned conventions here, dressing for dinner, but he was unprepared for the impact of seeing her when he knocked on the door of the room next to his to escort her back downstairs.

Avery had dressed in a calf-length gown of some ice-blue material that draped and floated over her body, the almost Grecian lines of it exposed the top curve of her breasts and the delicacy of her collarbone and shoulders. He was hard-pressed not to push her straight back into her room and onto the four-poster bed behind her. His hands curled into fists at his sides as he forced himself not to reach for her but he had far less control over the rest of his body and he felt his blood heat and thicken, thrumming with a slow deep pulse that sent desire southward.

"Shall we?" he said, offering her his arm—all too aware of her slender fingers as they rested on the fine cloth of his dinner jacket.

"I'm glad you could come with me," she said as they negotiated their way down the massive sweeping staircase that led to the ground floor.

Before he could respond, they were greeted by several of the other guests who'd already assembled. It wasn't long before Avery was swept up in a dance of greeting everyone and introducing him. He couldn't help but notice how, despite all the hugs and air kisses, she looked more embattled and beleaguered than welcomed. Here and there he caught snippets of conversation. Nothing he could call snide, but certainly not a hundred-percent friendly, either.

Obviously there were many here tonight who had known Avery through her family, and she was far more relaxed among them, but it wasn't long before he started to sense a theme in the conversation of the people who called themselves her friends. Each of them had expressed condolences on the loss of her father, but they'd also hastened to say how much they were looking forward to her being back in the swing of things. It didn't take a rocket scientist to figure out just how many of them were using her—either as a meal ticket to a good night out or for other reasons. He lost count of the number of times somebody asked her to introduce them to someone else.

Sure, he got the idea of networking. He was adept at it himself. He sure hadn't got where he was today without becoming a grand master at it. But when it came to Avery he began to feel annoyed at how she was letting herself be used by these people.

"Is there anyone here who is actually your friend?" he asked after she had introduced one particularly acerbic young woman to a man Marcus recognized as the CEO of one of the major banking corporations.

"Ouch," Avery said mockingly. "You think I don't have any friends?"

"That's not what I meant, and you know it. It just feels like everyone here has an ulterior motive and they're all using you to get what they want."

"And aren't we all doing that?" Avery asked quietly. "They're here to support my charity so I have an ulterior motive also, wouldn't you say?" She smiled and shrugged those graceful shoulders. "It's all part of the game, Marcus. Don't tell me you haven't played it yourself. We do what we must."

She was drawn away by their hostess to greet some newcomers and Marcus found himself leaning against a colonnade and sipping his glass of French champagne alone, Avery's words echoing in his head. *We do what we must.* And wasn't he doing what he must do? Doing what he owed his grandfather for the sacrifices the old man had made for him? Didn't the end, in his case, justify the means?

But as hard as he tried to convince himself he wasn't like the sycophants who'd clustered around Avery for the better part of the evening, he couldn't deny that he was equally guilty, and the truth didn't sit comfortably on his shoulders. He knew she was attracted to him—her reaction in the pool the other morning was nothing if not incendiary—and he knew her type. She didn't get involved in a physical liaison just for the fun of it. She was the kind of woman who gave everything when she gave herself—heart and soul. He didn't do love. It wasn't part of his plan.

Love had seen his mother blinded to his father's faults. Had seen her addicted to drugs and had seen her take the fall for his father during a deal gone bad. Love had destroyed her. He didn't want to hurt Avery and he knew, deep down, if they embarked upon an affair it was inevitable that he would.

If only she'd agree to sell the collection, he could then arrange to buy *Lovely Woman* anonymously and walk away before he inadvertently broke her heart.

Seven

Avery surreptitiously watched from across the table as Marcus chatted with the people who'd been seated around him at the formal dinner. He did so with incredible flair, charming the matrons, impressing the older gentlemen and clearly gathering a fan following of his own among the younger women and certainly some of the not so young. Yet every now and then he'd lift his gaze and search the room for her, nodding slightly and giving her a faint smile when their eyes would meet. It gave Avery a warm feeling deep inside. A feeling that finally began to chase away the darkness that had filled her since her father's death.

That she desired Marcus was a given. Every time she saw him her heart hammered a little faster in her chest, her nerve endings became that much more attuned to his every move. It only took the brush of his hand against hers while they had stood talking, earlier, to send an electrical zing through her body. But it went beyond the physical. Despite his air of polish she sensed that there was something about him, something that he tried to guard so carefully, that made her want to understand him more.

She thought about what had brought Marcus into her life and wondered if she was doing the right thing in holding out on selling the collection. In all honesty, what was she really hanging on to? An assembly of canvasses by Impressionist masters added to over the years by an avid collector. And why had her father collected them? The answer was simple, because of the joy they gave him.

Ted Wells's words came back to haunt her. Did she really think her father loved her any less than the works of art? When she examined her feelings truthfully she had to admit that, deep down, she knew her father had loved her. She also knew that, as the image of her mother, seeing her on a daily basis had only reinforced for him the loss they'd both endured when her mother had passed away. Holding on to the collection wouldn't make a difference to the past, it wouldn't change her childhood. If anything, letting it go would honor her father's memory and his acumen in assembling the collection as he had.

As Avery reached for her wineglass and took a sip of the excellent vintage from the castle's enviable cellars she realized she'd made a decision. And that decision filled her with an excitement she had rarely felt before. She would release the collection for sale. It was the right thing to do. And Marcus Price was the right man to represent it. Now, she just needed to find the right time to tell him.

It was late on Saturday evening before they returned to Avery's Kensington home. The silent auction of the children's work had been an outstanding success and, combined with the proceeds of the gala dinner the night before, the charity was well funded for the coming year. Avery fought back a yawn as they approached her house.

"Tired?" Marcus asked, lifting one hand from the steering wheel to stroke the back of her hand.

"A bit," she admitted.

Although last night had been a late one by her usual standards, it was her excitement over her decision to sell the collection that had kept her awake through the night. Concentrating on the setup for the auction this morning had been a welcome distraction as she tried to work out the best time to let Marcus know of her decision. To her it was so momentous she didn't want to just blurt it out, and she wanted him to know that she trusted him implicitly to do the very best job he could.

Already she had an idea for the funds the sale would raise. While the charity that had benefited from this weekend's dinner and auction was well set up, it rented spaces for the children in various communities. What if the charity had purpose-designated buildings at its disposal? Her mind had boggled at the idea, her thoughts expanding to the additional number of children whose talent they'd be able to foster with more dedicated space.

Once they were inside her house, Avery decided the time was right to give Marcus her news. Their bags had been taken up to their rooms and Mrs. Jackson had arranged a light supper for them in one of the downstairs parlors.

When they'd finished their meal and each were relaxing over a glass of wine, Avery took the bit in her teeth.

"Marcus, I've been thinking," she started.

"About the statue? Look, I'm sorry we haven't been able to turn anything new up for you yet but I'm still hopeful that at least one of the feelers I've put out will bring us a reward."

She shook her head. "No, it's not that. I've made a final decision about Dad's collection."

Marcus put his wineglass down carefully on the table beside him and faced her. She could see the tension in his face—the hope that warred with the anticipated disappointment.

"And that would be?" he prompted.

"I've decided to sell, and I'd like you, and Waverly's, to handle the sale for me."

He let go an audible breath and Avery searched his face for an expression of triumph. Instead there was nothing. His expression was as unreadable to her as a Sanskrit script.

"You're certain about this?" he asked.

A flare of irritation burned inside her. Wasn't this what he wanted? Hadn't he harangued her on the phone and by email for months for this very result? Why wasn't he happier about it?

"Of course I'm certain. It makes good sense for it to be available to people who would appreciate the art."

"You could do that by loaning it to a gallery or a museum," he pointed out, still with that neutral expression on his face.

"I thought you wanted to sell it. Have *you* changed your mind?" she demanded, getting up to pace the floor in her frustration.

Marcus rose from his seat and put his hands out to grab her shoulders, turning her to face him.

"I haven't changed my mind, but I am curious about why you've changed yours. I won't deny it, Avery. Selling your father's collection would be a career milestone for me, but I want you to be doing it because you're ready."

"If I wasn't ready I wouldn't have said I was," she said, still annoyed that he hadn't acted as if he was overjoyed to get the commission. "I've been thinking about it and I realized my reasons for holding on to the paintings weren't as important as I thought they were."

"What reasons were they?" he coaxed, his hands drifting from her shoulders to her upper arms and then back again.

"You probably understand as well as anybody how much that collection meant to my father. Adding to it consumed him for years. When he decided to release the occasional piece, he only did so after much deliberation and soul-searching, not to mention after vetting the prospective buyer thoroughly. He could tell you everything about each painting, right down to the last brush stroke. He loved them like they were his babies."

She saw understanding dawn in Marcus's eyes and she hated that he understood and could see her vulnerability so easily.

"You think he loved them more than he loved you?"

"I used to, yes. Somehow, holding on to the collection made me feel as if I was closer to him." She drew in a shuddering breath before continuing. "I'm sure a psychologist would have a field day with me but it took something Ted said the other day to make me realize that keeping the paintings didn't serve anyone, least of all me."

"Ted?"

"The gardener. I barely know the guy, and yet he could give me more insight in a few minutes than I had the sense to find myself in the months since Dad died."

"Sometimes it's easier for someone on the outside to see the big picture," Marcus said, pulling her against his chest and wrapping his arms around her.

It felt right to be here in his arms. Safe. And all too tempting. She rested her cheek against his chest, inhaling his scent deep into her lungs, listening to the steady beat of his heart and allowing herself to calm to the rhythm of his body.

"So are you going to accept my offer to represent the collection?" she asked. "Or should I approach someone else?"

She felt the muscles of his chest stiffen beneath her cheek, then relax once more as he realized she was only teasing him.

"Of course I will. I can go over the contract now if you like."

She shook her head slightly. "No, not right now. Don't worry, though, I won't change my mind. There's something else I want to ask of you."

"Something else? What's that?"

"Will you make love to me?"

* * *

Marcus heard a buzzing sound in his ears and realized he had yet to take a breath. He lifted a hand to stroke the side of Avery's face, pushing aside a wisp of hair.

"Are you certain?"

She smiled. "Do you really not trust me to know my own mind? Seems to me you have a lot of questions tonight, when you really should be taking action."

He laughed, hardly daring to believe his luck. First the collection, now this. He was no man's fool and he wasn't about to look a gift horse in the mouth, especially not one as beautiful as Avery.

"You're right. I'm an idiot. But never let it be said that I need to learn my lessons twice," he growled before taking her lips in a searing kiss.

She gave as good as she got, pushing her hands into his short hair and holding him to her as if she was a woman drowning. As if he were the beginning and the end of all her hopes and dreams. The responsibility of it threatened to overwhelm him. While his earlier research had proven she was known on the social circuit, she'd had a sheltered upbringing and she definitely wore her emotions close to the surface. He'd avoided women like her before, mentally tagging them as too needy for his tastes—but then never before had he been so captivated. By taking her to bed, he was stepping into uncharted territory.

The taste of her was intoxicating and reason soon fell to the back of his mind as her tongue traced the shape of his lips before brushing against his own. She allowed him entry to her mouth, suckling at his tongue in a way that sent an aching throb of desire straight to his groin. A throb that set up an insistent beat through his veins.

Reluctantly Marcus withdrew from her embrace, catching one of her hands in his. He wanted her with a fierce need he couldn't remember ever feeling before, but he wasn't going

to make their first time on a rug on a sitting-room floor—
no matter how priceless that hand-knotted rug might be. He
tugged her toward the door and they made it up the stairs
to his room where he shoved the door closed behind them.

Once there he took her in his arms again, backing her
slowly toward the bed, pulling her blouse from the waistband
of her skirt as he did so, his fingers fumbling as they fought
to unfasten her buttons. She was busy also, jerking his belt
loose from his trousers, before undoing the catch at his waist
and sliding his zipper down. And, then, oh, God, her hand
clasped him through his briefs. It was agony and pleasure in
one delectable grip.

From there, to naked, their actions were a blur. All he
knew was he had to get her on that bed, had to get inside her,
had to sate this near unquenchable need that drove him. Her
gasp as their legs tangled and they fell backward onto the bed
seared through his senses, reminding him of her fragility, her
softness. He hauled back on his desire, promising himself he
could slake his lust eventually, but not before he'd taken the
time to make sure she was with him every deliciously excru-
ciating step of the way.

His hands skimmed the gentle curve of her waist, up toward her rib cage and to the lower swell of her breasts. She
gasped anew as his fingertips toyed with her breasts, the soft
pink of her nipples deepening ever so slightly as the skin
puckered. He bent his head to one taut bud, teasing it with
the tip of his tongue before blowing a cool breath over the
moistened skin. She squirmed beneath him, a moan falling
from her lips, her hands fluttering to his shoulders, her nails
embedding in his skin. He welcomed the sensation, basking
briefly in the pleasure-pain of it before taking her nipple between his teeth and biting gently in response.

Her hips lifted off the bed, her mound brushing against
his erection and sending a jolt all the way up his spine. It
was enough to make him mindless but he couldn't let go to

his craving, not yet. He opened his mouth a little more, his tongue laving her nipple before drawing it into his mouth, suckling alternately hard, then soft before paying the same care and attention to her other breast.

Avery's body shook with tension, and he glided one hand down her body, over her hip and down her thigh before moving back up again. Again and again he touched her, his hands coming ever closer, yet never quite reaching, the center of her. He could feel her heat, smell the heady musky warmth of her, and when he let his fingers brush over her most sensitive bud her hands clutched convulsively at his shoulders once more.

"You're torturing me," she groaned.

"Would you like me to stop?" he teased.

"No, don't you dare!"

Marcus chuckled softly then dipped his head lower, letting his mouth, his tongue, traverse the same path his hand had taken. He didn't know for whom it was the most torment. Avery, with the way her body tautened and quaked, reaching for the release his touch promised to give her, or himself for all that his body implored him to simply take her and plunge them both into the maelstrom of pleasure that awaited just strokes away. It was the goal of that mutual satisfaction that kept him focused, that kept him from losing control. He wanted to make this as good as he possibly could for her— better than anything she'd experienced before.

He nuzzled the fine thatch of blond hair at the apex of her thighs before darting his tongue out to flick her clitoris. She didn't disappoint, her hips rose toward him and he grasped them with both hands, holding her firm, exactly where he wanted her. His tongue swirled around the pink pearl of nerve endings—once, twice—until he himself could take it no longer and he closed his mouth over her, suckling hard. He knew the exact moment she let go, felt the waves that crashed through her body, heard her scream of release as she bowed away from the bed, her body locked in a paroxysm of pleasure.

And with it, he could wait no longer. He quickly sheathed himself with a condom, thanking his foresight in putting a box in the bedside drawer, and raised himself over her body, positioned himself at her entrance and slid home. She was tight, almost painfully so, but eventually he felt her inner muscles relent to his invasion, felt the lingering pulse of her orgasm ease him farther inside. He tried to hold back, to take his time, but he couldn't wait another second. With the taste of her on his tongue, the feel of her hands on his body, and the tight sleeve of her body gripping his sex he felt himself pull back and surge forward again. And again. And again. Until there was no sense as to where he ended and Avery began. They were one in every sense of the physical realm.

Avery clutched at his shoulders, her nails digging into his skin but he barely felt it. His climax built with soaring speed, driving him harder, faster, until it swept him over the edge and onto wave after wave of satisfaction. He was aware of Avery joining him as his senses flew, the realization making his pleasure all the sweeter as her legs wrapped tight around his hips and her eyes glazed with fulfillment as a deep moan spilled from her lips. He rolled to one side, pulling her with him, their bodies still joined, their hearts still thumping at a frenetic pace.

"Oh…my…God," she said shakily, a shy smile wreathing her face.

"My thoughts exactly," he answered, equally breathless.

It was some minutes later before Marcus had the presence of mind to withdraw from her welcoming heat and get rid of the condom, his action garnering a faint protest from Avery as they disconnected.

"Come straight back," she ordered softly, a fresh promise already reflected in her eyes.

He kissed her briefly and rolled from the bed and headed to

the attached bathroom. Catching his reflection in the mirror he realized he looked like a very satisfied cat. To be honest, he couldn't believe his luck. Without coercion, Avery had not only come willingly into his arms but she'd also given him the biggest prize of his career—all in one evening. He could almost taste the champagne that would toast his elevation to partner at Waverly's already.

He quickly washed and dried his hands and turned off the light and headed back to the bed where he could see her lying bathed in moonlight. She looked almost otherworldly with her fair hair spread on the pillow, all color leached from her skin in the black and silver tones of the night.

She rose on one elbow as he approached. "Is everything okay?"

He smiled. "Everything's more than okay."

She reached for him as he slid onto the bed, her touch inciting his blood to fresh new heights, and he gave himself willingly over to her ministrations. As reserved as Avery was in public, she was the tangential opposite in private, and he was discovering he liked this side of her—very, very much.

Eight

They slept late Sunday morning, and Marcus woke to the gentle sensation of Avery's slender fingers tracing the shafts of sunlight that streaked through the partially opened curtain to stripe across his shoulders, and down his arms.

"I want to paint you," she said softly. "Like this, wearing no more than sunlight on your skin."

"Can we have breakfast first?" he asked, feeling his body respond even after the marathon lovemaking they'd shared last night.

She laughed and the sound thrilled him to his core. She was a far cry from the withdrawn and closed woman he'd met just over a week ago.

"Of course," she said, pushing their tumbled sheets aside. "I'll ask Mrs. Jackson to serve it in the studio."

"Tease," he retorted, reaching for her, but she evaded him and headed for the door leading to her private bathroom.

She paused, her hand on the doorknob, and he drank in

he sight of her naked form. Her sun-gilded skin so enticing, he untouched parts of her even more so.

"So? Are you hungry?" she taunted as she opened the door.

He caught a glimpse of her butt as she slipped inside the bathroom, heard her giggle in response to his roar.

It was quite some time before they made it into clothing and up to the next floor. Marcus's nose twitched at the scent of coffee—the silver pot sitting over a warmer on an ornately carved sideboard. He felt his lips pull back in a wry smile. Even with the income he pulled he'd never be able to touch the effortless old-money style Avery was so accustomed to.

She reached for a cup and saucer and poured his coffee, adding the requisite lumps of sugar for him without a second thought. As she handed it to him she said, "I've already decided what I'm going to do with the money from the sale of the collection."

She outlined her plans for the children's art charity and Marcus felt his anticipation lift by degrees. His mind raced ahead to what he would need to do next. He could barely believe it. He turned to face the painting he'd been waiting almost his lifetime to possess. *Lovely Woman* was finally within his grasp.

Making a deliberate effort to keep his voice level he said, "Sounds like you're well on the way to getting it organized. I'm looking forward to photographing and inventorying the collection myself. I can start with *Lovely Woman* later today if you're agreeable."

Avery's next words poured icy cold water on his plans. "Oh, no, she won't be part of the sale. The pieces I'm letting go are at the house in Los Angeles."

He forced himself to keep his voice light. "Are you sure that's a good move? This painting alone could keep your charity in supplies for the kids for years. I really think you should reconsider."

Despite his best efforts, some of his frustration must have

leached through in his voice because Avery took a step back
a small frown creasing between her eyebrows. He should have
known better. A woman like Avery needed to be coaxed gen
tly, to be seduced into agreement. He knew he could do it
Marcus thought, pushing aside the pang of guilt that plucked
at his chest. The end justified the means. It had to.

"I said she's not for sale and she's not," Avery said em
phatically. "Are you telling me the rest of the collection isn'
enough for Waverly's?"

"That's not it at all. But collectors are well aware of wha
your father had accumulated. There will be questions abou
why the consignment isn't complete." He couldn't back dow
straightaway.

Avery sniffed dismissively. "Well, it's as complete a:
they're going to get it. Besides, it's not as if this one is a tru
Impressionist since it was executed well after the period. Pur
ists wouldn't be interested."

He gave it one more try. "It's still in the Impressionist style
Avery. Logically it forms a part of the whole, don't you think'
Your father seemed to believe so or else, family connection
aside, why would he have included it in the collection?"

She didn't understand it. Why was Marcus so insistent o
including this painting in the sale items? He almost sounded
annoyed that it wasn't.

Avery walked over to the painting and wrapped her arm
around her stomach, holding herself tight. She'd lost he
mother, she'd lost her father. She'd agreed to sell the rest o
her father's paintings. Wasn't that enough? Did she have t
let everything go?

No. The answer echoed emphatically in her head. She di
not.

"Whatever his reasons, I'm keeping it because it's far mor
than a connection to just my father. It's a link to my fami
ly's past and proof of an appreciation of beauty that's bee

passed down through generations of Cullens in one form or another. She's not for sale and that's my final word on the subject, Marcus. Please respect that."

"I'm sorry, I didn't mean to upset you." Marcus came up behind her, his arms crossing over hers and pulling her back against the solid warmth of his chest.

Avery started to brush aside his apology but then she stopped herself. He *had* upset her. He'd been so dogged about it and it made her wonder why. It was just one picture out of a considerable set of collected works.

She felt the warmth of his breath at the back of her neck, a warmth soon followed by the press of his lips. She couldn't help it. A shiver of longing rippled through her at his touch.

"Forgive me?" he asked softly, tracking a line of short kisses from her neck and along the top edge of her shoulder.

Did she? She gave a little sigh. Of course she did. It wasn't as if he had an ulterior motive, after all. He was a businessman and he had a job to do. He'd made that clear from the outset. Obviously he felt it was in her best interests, and the charity's, to present the strongest consignment for sale.

"Yes, I do," she said, turning in the circle of his arms and meeting his lips with her own.

Everything between them was just fine, and she wanted it to stay that way.

"Are you still going to pose for me?" she asked.

"I tell you what," he said, reaching to pull his T-shirt up and over his head, exposing his torso in a movement that made a strong flick of desire whip through her body. "If I have to be naked, then you do, too."

A slow smile pulled at her lips. "I need to do some preliminary sketches first."

"Then there's no reason for you to be clothed, right?"

"I guess not," she admitted, feeling a flush of heat infuse her entire body at the thought.

"So what's holding you back?"

Avery tried to remain composed and distant as she dis
robed and reached for her sketchbook and pencils, but the
sight of Marcus lounging on the daybed wearing nothing
but an intense look on his face served as a major distraction.
She tore off the sheet she'd been drawing on, and attempted
to start anew, nibbling at the top of her pencil as she tried to
remain objective while she assessed her subject.

"Problem?" Marcus asked.

"Nothing I won't work out, eventually," she replied, ris
ing from her stool and putting her things down. "Maybe if
you posed like this—"

She reached across him to take his hand and drape his
arm along his side, his hand resting on his hip. As she did so,
he leaned forward slightly to give a short lick of his tongue
across her nipple. She'd been so aware of every inch of him
that his action made her shudder in response, heat and mois
ture flooding her core.

"How's that?" he asked.

"I think the pose, at least, is better," she said a little breath
lessly.

This was ridiculous. One touch and she was a molten mess
of aching need for him. She knew of only one cure for what
ailed her.

"Or maybe, this would be better," she said, rolling him on
to his back, his shoulders still propped by the mass of pillows
she'd arranged earlier.

Marcus said nothing, merely watching her behind half
lowered lids as she knelt beside the bed and trailed her hand
across his hip and down over the top of his thigh. She saw
his sex jerk a little as her hand moved nearer. Near, but not
close enough to touch him. She allowed her hand to continue
its journey down one leg before starting back up the other.

"Yes," she murmured, "this is much better."

He was fully erect now, the veins on his shaft prominent,
its head a ripe plum for the taking. She bent her head, her

braid falling forward to brush against the skin at the top of his thigh, in the indentation of where his hip arrowed to his groin. Looking up to meet his eyes she opened her mouth, moistened her lower lip with her tongue.

His entire body tensed, his eyes glittering like emeralds. She took him in her hand and licked him, from base to tip.

"How's that?" she asked, deliberately using his own words back at him.

He seemed to be beyond speech, his hands curled into fists at his side. She repeated the movement, this time closing her mouth over him when she reached his tip and drawing him into her mouth. Again she duplicated her action, this time taking him a little deeper, and again, and again, settling into a rhythm. He emitted a low hiss from between clenched teeth.

"Avery?"

"Hmm?" she replied, swirling her tongue around him, tasting the hint of his pleasure.

"You're killing me here," he groaned, pushing his head back against the pillows, the cords of his neck prominent.

"You're right, perhaps I should stop," she suggested, releasing him for a moment.

"No! Yes!"

"Which is it, Marcus?" She rose onto the bed, straddling his legs with her own, still holding him in her hand.

In response he reached for his jeans where they lay on the floor next to the bed. He dragged a condom from his pocket and ripped the packet open. He slid the protection over his aching flesh then grabbed Avery's hips, positioning her over him.

"Like this, now!"

It was astonishing the sense of power she felt poised over his body like this. She guided him to her core and lowered herself so she only took in the head of him before pulling up just that little bit. He groaned beneath her, his fingers tightening their grip but still allowing her the control. She bore down again, and this time the action sent a shock of exquisite sensation radiating from deep inside her.

Beads of perspiration formed on her upper lip as she fought the urge to sink lower, to take him fully inside. She hesitated, withdrew, then dropped upon him again. This time the jolt was even stronger, leaving her shaking with the effort to prolong things as much as she possibly could. Three more times she managed it before instinct overrode her need to take things slow. As if sensing she was at the breaking point, Marcus's hips thrust upward, meeting her on her downward stroke.

Color burst behind her eyes and she braced her hands on his chest, giving over to the tempo time immemorial demanded. She felt his release as an intense burst of heat and energy, the knowledge that she'd driven him to the brink and beyond sending her cascading over the edge into intense waves of ecstasy that threatened to rob her of consciousness.

Her body continued to pulse as she collapsed, sprawled across his chest. Somewhere along the line her braid had come undone and her hair spread across them both. It was unbelievable what he could do to her, how he could make her feel. She didn't want it to end, ever, but she knew he was only here for a short time and she wasn't going to waste it.

She opened her eyes, her gaze tracking straight across the room to *Lovely Woman,* the picture itself inspiring her to eventually pull herself from his arms and pick up her sketchbook and pencil again.

"Don't move," she ordered. "I want you just like that."

"You just had me like this," Marcus said with a lazy smile that made her stomach flip all over again.

She laughed and repeated her command, "Don't move."

Inspired anew by her subject, Avery's pencil flew across the paper and she moved around the room changing her angle several times before she was satisfied with the end result.

"I'm done," she said happily, throwing herself back down on the daybed beside him and showing him her drawings.

Marcus could see immediately that figures were Avery's milieu, backing up what she'd said that day in the garden when he'd commented on the landscape she was working on. In fact, her talent was very similar to that of her forebear, Baxter Cullen. During his studies Marcus had seen a selection of preliminary sketches Cullen had done, as well as the oils he'd been so well known for.

"These are good," he commented.

"You think so?"

She looked surprised to hear his praise. A thought occurred to him. "Have you ever shown your work?"

She shook her head. "I've mostly painted for my own pleasure, and donated the occasional piece for anonymous auction—you know, where people don't necessarily know whose work they're bidding on."

"I'm surprised. You should think about a show. I can arrange it for you if you like."

"Let me think about it, I...I don't know if I'm ready to put myself out there like that. I mostly paint for my own pleasure, and like this, with you—well, it's easy when it's a subject you love."

Marcus felt every cell in his body freeze. Did she just say she loved him? She didn't appear to realize her slip of the tongue, instead getting up and walking over toward *Lovely Woman*. He was mesmerized by the play of the light in the studio over her skin, and the way it emphasized her graceful gait and her slender form.

"I think Baxter must have loved her, don't you?"

Denial tore through him. Baxter Cullen had used Kathleen Price, or O'Reilly as she'd been then. He very much doubted love had been involved in any way, shape or form. Avery turned and looked at him, clearly expecting a response. He rose from the daybed and padded across the wooden floor to her side.

"What makes you think that?" he hedged.

"I don't know, it's just something in the way he's executed this. I don't see how he could have created something this beautiful without love very strong in his heart."

"Lust maybe," Marcus commented, "but love? I don't think so."

How could it have been love? Surely if Baxter Cullen had loved Kathleen he'd have stood up to his wife, or at the very least made provisions for Kathleen when she was summarily dismissed. No. The man had used a woman in a weaker position than himself. He'd taken advantage of his power, Marcus was sure of it. From what his grandfather had said, Kathleen Price had been a woman of honor and integrity—certainly not the type to become some rich man's plaything. She'd worked herself to the bone to support her family, marrying late and bearing only one child as a result. She was not the sort of woman to submit to a dalliance with an older married man so out of her class. She'd had scruples, which was more than Marcus could say for her employer.

"Can't you see it? I think it's there in every stroke of his brush. Like this," she said, touching the round of his shoulder, "and this." She traced along his collarbone.

Marcus grabbed her hand in his, pressing it against his cheek. "You're romanticizing what is simply a brilliantly executed piece of art."

Avery looked at him—and was that pity in her eyes?

"Oh, Marcus. Sometimes you have to look past the technique and the media, and look into the soul of a painting."

"I'd rather look at you," he murmured, gathering her close and kissing her, deliberately distracting her from something he knew he could never agree with her on.

That night as they made love again, this time slow and languorous and without the soul-burning intensity of earier in the day, there was no mistaking Avery's cry when she climaxed.

"I love you, Marcus!"

The short sentence rang in his ears, stroking his guilt yet at the same time touching a part of him that warmed to the words, that wanted to be able to accept them, but knew he couldn't. Because no matter what, one day soon he would have to walk away from Avery Cullen, and when he did, he wanted to be certain he had *Lovely Woman* with him.

Nine

Avery walked in the garden alone. Marcus was attending to more Waverly's business and while she didn't begrudge him that, she did miss him. It had become too easy to get used to his presence, to become addicted to his lovemaking. She'd never considered herself an especially sensual woman, but somehow, in Marcus's arms, she had become a wanton. She knew her declaration of love two nights ago had surprised him, she'd felt him change—not withdraw from her, exactly but he was different.

It was probably her fault for using the *L* word so soon. A man like Marcus, well, he was a man of the world and, despite all her wealth and privilege, she'd had a pretty sheltered life. Sure she'd hit the party scene with her friends for a while the party scene they still tried to lure her back to. But she knew that life wasn't for her. What was important to her wa family, a home, surrounding herself with the people and the things she loved and trusted.

Could Marcus love her? she wondered. Or deep down

was he still using her? She smiled as she thought of the way they'd used each other at dawn before he'd had to dress and catch a flight to Manchester to visit a potential client. When she thought about it, she supposed everyone used somebody once in a while. She was used to it—had even convinced herself she didn't mind it, or at least could live with it. But with Marcus it was different. She wanted him to want her every bit as deeply as she wanted him, and she wasn't talking in the physical sense, either.

He'd sat for her again yesterday so she could start on his oil painting. Once more, he'd tried to bring up the subject of *Lovely Woman* and once more she'd shut him down. What was with his obsession with selling it? Couldn't he just accept she wasn't going to let the painting go, not for love or money?

"You look as if you've got a lot on your mind."

Ted Wells's voice interrupted her thoughts.

"Oh, yes. I've got plenty to think about at the moment. By the way, I took your advice about Dad's collection. I'm letting Waverly's represent it."

"Are you happy with your decision? You can change your mind, you know."

"Yeah, I know." She nodded her head. "I'm okay with it. But I'm keeping one of the paintings for myself. It's the only one that means something to me, but Marcus thinks I should still include it."

Ted shrugged. "I don't see why you should if you don't want to. So how're things going with young Price? Mrs. Jackson mentioned you two are spending a whole lot of time together lately."

Avery blushed. The last time she'd spoken to Ted, and that wasn't all that long ago, she'd only just met Marcus. Now, here she was, mooning around the garden thinking about him—no doubt wearing her heart on her sleeve.

"Things are okay," she said, unable to stop the smile that spread across her face. "He's helping me with the statue like you suggested. I'm not sure that he's making much more headway than I did myself but I know he's trying. It's just his doggedness about *Lovely Woman* that bothers me, I guess."

"A man like Marcus Price didn't get where he is now without being very ambitious," Ted observed.

"I know, and when he's not talking work he's great to be with." She couldn't keep the warmth from her voice.

"You sound quite taken with him."

"I am, in fact, I actually think I've fallen in love. Can it happen like that, Ted? Have you ever fallen in love so fast it left you dizzy?"

Ted smiled, the action creasing his handsome weathered face. "Yeah, I have and I've always said you gotta follow your heart."

The rest of the week passed uneventfully, with the exception of a succession of blissful nights spent in Marcus's arms, she thought with a private smile.

He was busy on the phone today, coordinating having an approved Waverly's photographer to document the collection in Los Angeles in preparation for the Waverly's catalog. David Hurley, her assistant, had sent through the requisite information complete with condition report, provenance and most recent valuation for each painting. He'd also liaised with David on the packing company that would crate and ship the canvases to New York.

Avery also had been busy. She'd set in motion discussions with the children's charity about the additional trust to be set up to hold the buildings she planned to buy with the proceeds from the sale. The lawyers would no doubt get fat on all the legal requirements involved but at the same time she knew she was doing the right thing for the children.

She'd invited Marcus along with her to the gallery opening she'd been asked to attend tonight, but he'd cried off saying he wanted to make the most of the time difference between

London and L.A. to talk with David. Now, she was just about ready to head out the door. As part of their VIP treatment, the gallery was sending a driver for her so at least she didn't have to worry about parking. She popped her head into the study to say goodbye to Marcus on her way out.

"Wow, maybe I should come with you after all," Marcus said, coming out from behind the desk the second he saw her.

Avery was filled with that delicious melting sensation she got every time she saw him. She did a little twirl, the action showing off her legs in the deep rose-pink silk crepe and organza party dress she'd bought for tonight.

"Are you worried someone might sweep me away?" she teased.

"Let them try and they'll have me to deal with," he said darkly.

Her breath caught in her throat. This was the closest he'd come to actually saying she was his. As far as she was concerned, no other man would exist in the room tonight. Her heart was firmly here at home with Marcus, but could she begin to hope he felt the same way about her?

"I'll be sure and give them your number," Avery said, forcing the same light tone into her voice that she'd used a moment ago.

"Yeah," Marcus growled, catching her hand and dragging her to him. "Make sure you do that so I can warn them all off."

A chime at the front door alerted them to her driver's arrival.

"I'd better go."

"You'll have to fix your lipstick," Marcus said.

"It's okay, oh—"

Marcus took her mouth in a long wet kiss that left her in no doubt that he was looking forward to her return.

"I can stay home," she offered, her blood already heated, her body craving his. "I'll send the driver away."

"As tempting as that is, I really need to work." He turned

her around and gave her a gentle push in the direction of the door. "Go, have a good time, but not too good, okay?"

Avery repaired her lipstick in the car, but still had a smile on her face when she arrived at the gallery. There was already quite a throng and she accepted a glass of champagne from one of the passing waiters with her usual thanks before circulating through the rooms and greeting those she knew. The works on display weren't her cup of tea, too dark and violent. In fact, some of them made her even feel slightly ill. She'd do what she needed to do and then she'd head home, she decided, leaving her untouched champagne on a side table and reaching for a small bottle of sparkling mineral water instead.

"Avery! Long time no see."

She turned and forced herself to paint a smile on her lips. "Peter Cameron, how lovely to see you. What brings you to London?"

She leaned forward for the obligatory air kiss that sufficed for greeting between acquaintances but was left slightly off balance when he connected with her cheek, right beside her mouth. That certainly hadn't been an accident, she thought, fighting the urge to wipe away the imprint his touch had left.

"Promotion, what else?" The man laughed. "I'm with Rothschild's, at their West End offices now."

The last time she'd seen Peter had been in L.A. when he'd unrelentingly pursued her. As a date he wasn't entirely unappealing but there'd been an edge to him that had instinctively put her guard up.

"Missing the sunshine and beaches yet?" she asked, looking over his shoulder at a clock on the wall and hoping it wouldn't be considered too rude if she left soon.

"Not yet," he admitted. "I've got enough to keep me busy although I don't know how I'll cope with a British winter. What are you doing here in London?"

"I moved over to be with my dad while he was ill—I've decided to stay here, make this my permanent home."

"Hey, yeah, sorry to hear about your loss." Peter brushed past the condolences. "Since we're in the same city we should catch up. What about dinner tomorrow night?"

Avery pushed back the feeling of revulsion that built in her stomach as he took her hand and squeezed. She gently disengaged it from his hold and shook her head.

"No, thank you. I'm with someone."

"Ah, so the rumors are true." Peter looked displeased. "Tell me, do I know him?"

"You might," she said with a light shrug. "He works for your opposition. Marcus Price."

Peter let out a low whistle. "And wasn't he quick on the uptake. He's a bit of a charmer, our Marcus. I suppose he's sweet-talked you out of the Cullen Collection, too."

Was that sour grapes talking? One of the reasons Peter had tried so often to meet her father while he was still alive was to sound him out about whether or not he'd ever part with the collection.

"I think that's privileged information," she hedged.

Peter gave her a salacious wink. "What happens between the sheets, stays between the sheets. It's okay, I understand. But you should seriously consider putting the collection with Rothschild's. I can *personally* guarantee we'll do a far better job."

A bitter taste flooded across her tongue at his insinuation and fury at his attitude warred with long-instilled manners. Thankfully, manners won. There were enough paparazzi here tonight to have a field day if she lost her temper.

"Look, it's been lovely, but I really have to head off. Another engagement," she fibbed. Well, being with Marcus was another engagement in her book anyway.

"Give my regards to Marcus," Peter said with a marked lack of sincerity.

"Sure," Avery said, keen now to get away. Talking about

Marcus to Peter was distasteful—as if Peter's tarnish could rub off on their fledging relationship.

"Nice to see the guy has come to some success although I doubt you'll ever be able to completely knock the rough edges off him."

"Rough edges?" She had no idea what he was talking about.

"I heard he clawed his way to where he is now the hard way. Blue-collar origins, brought up by his grandfather after his mother died in prison of a drug overdose. They even say his grandfather bought off the father so he'd never touch Marcus again. I bumped into a few of his old private-school friends. They said he was driven even then. Scholarships of course."

"Of course," Avery repeated, feeling nothing but respect for Marcus.

In fact, if she could have loved him more at that minute she did. Marcus *had* come up the hard way. He hadn't enjoyed the easy glide through life that came with everything being served on a twenty-four-carat gold platter as she'd experienced her entire life.

"Still keen on your Waverly's hotshot?" Peter asked, his voice revealing that snaky side of him she'd never quite trusted. "He's driven. He'll do whatever it takes to get what he wants. I tell you, bring your business to Rothschild's. You won't regret it."

"Actually, I don't believe that Rothschild's and I would be a good fit. I've always been taught you need to respect the people you do business with."

Her put-down did little to deter him. But that was a measure of the kind of man Cameron was.

"Don't knock it till you've tried it," he responded with a leer. "Whatever Marcus can do for you, Avery, I promise I'll do it better."

His sly innuendo made her feel physically ill. She had to

get away from him before she embarrassed herself all over his well-shined shoes.

"I'd say it's been a pleasure, but it hasn't. Good night."

Not to be put off by her quelling goodbye, Cameron was determined to have the last word. "Mud sticks, Avery. Remember that. And there's got to be more dirt in Price's background. I'll be sure to let you know when I find it."

She turned and fled, not even waiting for the major domo stationed at the door to summon her driver, instead waving down one of London's ubiquitous cabs and diving inside as if her sanity depended on it. As she settled back in the cracked upholstery and gave her details to the driver she realized she was shaking. She'd never liked Peter Cameron but right now she actively loathed him.

She weighed the information he'd shared with her with what she already knew about Marcus. Yes, it was clear he was driven, and if Peter's information had been correct and Marcus had made his way through private school and college with scholarships it spoke volumes about his tenacity and focus. She'd experienced a bit of that tenacity herself, she thought with a smile. Where would she be now if he hadn't taken "no" for an answer when she'd spurned his requests to discuss the Cullen Collection?

A great deal lonelier—that was a fact. She couldn't wait to get home. Driven or not, Marcus Price was the man who held her heart and she couldn't wait to show him, again, just how much.

Ten

After her experience at the gallery with Cameron, Avery was glad she had no additional functions she needed to attend over the weekend. Besides which, she was feeling more tired than usual. Mind you, that probably had a great deal to do with the lack of sleep she'd been having lately. Marcus was a driven man, in work and in play. And, if the past couple of weeks were anything to go by, he liked to excel at whatever it was that he was doing.

However much he excelled, he had yet to find any trace of the angel statue, and Avery knew his lack of progress on the matter frustrated him. He wasn't a man accustomed to failure. She thought about his background, how he'd obviously worked so hard alongside those with a greater sense of privilege than he'd enjoyed. She'd broached the subject of his upbringing with him on Sunday night, but he'd been short and to the point, saying only that he'd been extremely lucky that his grandfather had brought him up and that he owed him a great deal for it.

She'd almost finished his nude, a project that had progressed far quicker than her garden painting had, that was for sure. She was just adding a few touches here and there when she heard Marcus come into the room.

"I've brought you coffee and lunch," he said, putting a tray on the sideboard.

"Thanks," she answered, putting down her brush and wiping her hands quickly on a cloth. "I think I'm done with the painting."

"That's great," Marcus said, pouring her a mug of coffee from the carafe he'd brought upstairs to her.

Avery took the mug from him and raised the fragrant brew to her lips, ready to take that first reenergizing morning mouthful, but the liquid never made it to her mouth. Instead her stomach turned at the prospect of sipping it.

"Has Mrs. Jackson changed the coffee beans?" she asked, taking another sniff and feeling the same awful reaction.

"I don't think so." Marcus took the mug from her and sipped. "Still tastes the same. Would you rather I ring for another pot?"

"No, that's okay. I'll stick with water this morning. Probably better for me anyway." She grabbed one of the bottles of water she always kept on hand in the studio and twisted the cap off, taking a long drink in an attempt to rid herself of the lingering aftereffect of smelling the coffee.

"I just had a call from my PA," Marcus said, helping himself to one of the club sandwiches on the tray.

"Oh, she's up early, isn't she?"

"I'm lucky, Lynette's dedicated to her work. To be honest, the woman terrifies me she's that organized. She's been at Waverly's for thirty years."

"Wow, that is dedication."

"Hmm, yeah. There's not much she doesn't know about the firm, that's for sure. Anyway, she called to let me know there's a special evening organized for Tuesday night, and reminded me that my attendance is expected."

"Tomorrow?" Avery asked. "Do you have to go?"

She could feel herself missing him already.

"I do, but I was hoping you'd come with me. I hope you don't mind but I asked Lynette if she could book us both on the 10:00 a.m. flight out of Heathrow tomorrow morning. That way we'll be landing at J.F.K. around one and that'll give us some time to rest before the party. What do you say?"

What did she say? She loved the idea. As far as she knew she had no pressing engagements to keep her here in London over the next few days. But first and foremost in her mind was that she didn't have to say goodbye to him just yet. It warmed her to her soul that he wanted her to come with him. Even that he wanted her to attend the party with him tomorrow night.

"That sounds great," she replied with a smile. "I can pack this afternoon."

"Good," Marcus said. "Make sure you pack for a week or so, if you can spare being away that long. I'm expecting the collection to come in next weekend and I'd like to be there when it's inventoried. Then we can think about when we can put it in the schedule and organize the presale exhibition."

"Wow, you're moving fast on this," she commented.

"No reason to delay, is there?"

"No, not at all." She heard the edge in his voice. "Don't worry, Marcus, I haven't changed my mind about selling."

"Are you sure? There's still time to include her." He gestured to *Lovely Woman*.

"I meant I am not about to withdraw those paintings I've agreed to sell." She shook her head slightly. Maybe it was time to nail down why he was so stubborn about including her great-great-uncle's painting. "Look, you keep going on about it, how about you tell me exactly why you're so persistent about including her."

* * *

If he told her the truth, would she give in? He doubted it. He opted for a vague version of the truth.

"I know of at least one potential buyer who would pay handsomely for the painting."

"Well, your buyer is set to be sadly disappointed, then, aren't they," she said adamantly. "And I'd appreciate it if you'd drop the subject. I'm not budging, Marcus."

He bit back the frustration that threatened to verbalize on his tongue. He owed her more than that. She'd been amazing these past couple of weeks and he needed to respect her decision about *Lovely Woman* no matter how much it killed him inside to do so. Still, he hadn't given up hope that she might change her mind. She'd changed her mind about the rest of the Cullen Collection, after all. Unfortunately, time was running out.

"Tenacity is my middle name," he said with a self-deprecating smile, "but okay, I'll drop the subject."

"Promise me, Marcus. You forget, I've seen just how tenacious you can be," Avery said, smiling in return and giving him a playful push.

In response he caught her hand and dragged her up against his body. Arousal came hot and fast. "Are you complaining, Miss Cullen?"

She rolled her hips against his erection. "What do you think?" she murmured against his lips.

"I think that perhaps I need to *show* you just how tenacious I can be. Just as a reminder for future reference."

His hands gripped the edge of her T-shirt and lifted it high, dragging the soft well-washed fabric over her head and dropping it to the ground. With the back of his knuckle he brushed the tops of her breasts, delighting in how the skin tautened beneath his touch. He bent to kiss her, his tongue tracing the enticing scalloped lace edge of her bra, dipping in past the demi-cup to stroke against her nipples.

Avery shuddered beneath his touch, her knees buckling a little and her breath audibly catching in her throat. She hummed a long sound of satisfaction when his hand crept around her back to unfasten her bra and then slid the shoulder straps down her arms until the garment joined her top on the floor.

Her nipples were tight pink puckered buttons and he laved first one, then the other. She laced her fingers at the back of his head, holding him to her, silently encouraging him to give more. And give more he did. He cupped her breasts in both hands, burying his face in their fullness, massaging them gently in response to her moan of pleasure. When he took one nipple in his mouth and suckled she gripped his hair tight. He suckled again, the fingers of his other hand teasing and tweaking her other nipple at the same time.

"Marcus, you're driving me crazy."

"That was my plan," he said, smiling against her creamy skin, tracing a blue vein with the tip of his tongue before straightening and scooping her up into his arms.

She squealed in surprise, flinging her hands around his neck. "Put me down, I'm too heavy," she protested.

If only she knew, he thought. Wanting her gave him a strength that made carrying her a pleasure, not a burden. He walked across the studio to the daybed and quickly stripped her of the rest of her clothes.

"You have me at a disadvantage, Mr. Price," Avery said from beneath lowered lids. Her gaze an alluring come-on.

"I find myself wanting to paint you," he replied, reaching for one of her watercolor brushes from the stack on the table nearby.

He'd loved the way she'd organized her studio. She was a little neat freak about the way she put things in their places and he found that trait endearing in the extreme.

"Paint me? I thought you said painting wasn't your forte."

"It's not, but I think I can do this," he said with a smile, filling a jar with water and making his way back to her side. "Now lie completely still, like a good model, and let me work. You know how temperamental we artists can get when we're disturbed."

She had a small smile on her face, as if she was indulging him, but when he moistened the brush and brought it down in a sensual sweep along her collarbone the smile fled.

"Ah, yes," he said. "Emphasizing the play of light on your body is indeed the most important part of this work of art. The way your skin is radiant here, yet changes here—" he stroked his brush lower, across the outside edge of the fullness of one breast and then along the underside "—is quite entrancing. It entices a man to want to touch, to taste and feel."

"W-why don't you do that?" she stammered.

He smiled back in return. A flush of desire had lit bright spots on her cheeks, her upper chest now a blush of pink. "Eventually, I have to finish my painting first."

She began to tremble as he applied the same technique to her other breast, a tiny cry falling from her lips as he swirled the brush across her nipples, leaving them wet and glistening in the early afternoon sun that streamed in through the windows. It was all he could do not to rip his clothes off, and sheath himself in her body. To give her what every touch, every caress promised. But he forced himself to hold back, to remain in rigid control. *Rigid* being the operative word, he thought as he paused in his work to adjust himself. It was useless though, his desire for her had him raging hard. There was only one thing that would assuage this fire.

Avery was shaking by the time his brush traced the shadowed lines at the tops of her thighs that led to her innermost femininity. Her body jumped as his brush swept across her clitoris, her hands suddenly reaching for his. "Please, Marcus."

"When you ask so nicely, how can I refuse," he said softly, bending down to follow the wet trail of the brush with his tongue. "There, is that better?" he said, pausing to look up at her face.

Her eyes glittered like shards of blue ice. "You like making me suffer?" she gasped.

"Suffer? No. Suffering is touching you, and not having you touch me."

She sat upright, her hands flying to his belt and hastily dragging his zipper down. The rasp of the tongue over the teeth of the zipper was nearly his undoing but then in an instant she'd freed him from his confines, her delicate fingers wrapping around the smoothness of his shaft and squeezing—at first gentle, then with more grip. It was all he could do not to lose control.

"Give me a second," he demanded and pulled free of her before standing and tearing away his clothes. He paused only long enough to grab a small packet from his trouser pocket and to rip it open and protect them both.

Then, thank God, he was nestled between her beautiful long legs. Legs that curled up and around his hips, holding him steady as with a shaking hand he held himself poised at her entrance. He could feel the heat of her body, could see how wet and ready she was for him. He slowly slid inside all the way, and stopped there, taking a moment to relish the delicious sensation of her holding him like a custom-made glove. Then primal instinct took control and he began to pump his hips. He was already close, so very close.

He bent his head to press a hot wet kiss to her lips, trying to slow his actions for just long enough to regain control. He traced the cord of her neck with the tip of his tongue, down across her collarbone and in a line toward one tightly beaded nipple. He drew her into his mouth, his teeth abrading her sensitive skin before suckling against her. Her body went stiff and he felt the ripples begin inside her. Ripples that strengthened and spread until she called out his name on a wrenching cry. Ripples that dragged him into blissful oblivion that seemed

:o come from the soles of his feet and spread throughout his body with an intensity that almost brought tears to his eyes.

He collapsed on top of her, barely able to breathe let alone think. But one surety echoed in his mind. He didn't want to let Avery Cullen go—ever.

The early start to get to the airport in time to check in for their flight left Avery feeling strangely drained the next morning and she slept for most of the journey across the Atlantic. After they'd cleared customs and immigration at J.F.K. Marcus hailed a cab, which whisked them into the city and his apartment. Avery was curious to see how he lived. He seemed to fit so well in her world, she was intrigued to find out if she'd be as comfortable in his.

She'd picked him for a brownstone kind of guy so she was surprised when they pulled up outside an anonymous-looking apartment building in Chelsea. Marcus paid the cabdriver and rolled their suitcases to the entrance where a liveried doorman held the door open for him.

"Good afternoon, Mr. Price. I trust your trip to London was successful and you had a good flight home?"

"Thanks, Buck, it was great. This is my guest, Miss Cullen. She'll be staying with me so I hope you'll look after her."

"I will indeed, sir. Welcome to New York, Miss Cullen."

"Thank you," Avery said with an inclination of her head. It was nice to know that Marcus wasn't faceless where he lived. "It's always good to be here."

A short elevator ride took them to the eighth floor where Marcus led her to his apartment. He pushed open the door and held it for her.

"Welcome to my humble abode," he said. "It's a bit smaller than you're used to but I think you'll be comfortable."

"It looks great," Avery said as she looked around while Marcus took their cases through to the master bedroom.

She followed him down the hall, noting here and there the occasional framed pen and ink drawing on the wall.

Marcus hefted her case onto the bed and turned to open the sliding door to the wardrobe, shoving aside some of his suits to make space for her. "You can hang your things here if you like, or in the spare room. There's room in the dresser too, just put all my stuff in the lower drawers."

"Are you sure?" she asked, unsure of the etiquette in a situation like this. Somehow it was something neither her father nor any of her nannies had ever covered.

"Yeah, you don't want to be living out of a suitcase. I'll go get us something to eat while you unpack."

"Thanks, I'm starved." It had been way too early for her to eat breakfast when they'd left London and she'd slept through most of the meal service on the flight.

"I thought you might be. Omelet okay?"

She faked a swoon of delight.

"I'll get on to it, then," he said, leaving her alone.

It felt odd to be hanging up her clothing alongside his in the wardrobe. Odd, yet at the same time right. Or was she just clinging to straws? No words of love had passed his lips and it wasn't as if an invitation to share his wardrobe and dresser drawers was an invitation to share his life. She was just being more fanciful than usual.

With businesslike efficiency she emptied the top drawer of his dresser, rearranged things for him in the lower drawer and put away the rest of her things into the top drawer. Her vanity bag she took through to the bathroom and propped it upon the almost-bare charcoal-gray marble top. Marcus's apartment might be sparer than she'd anticipated, but everything was of excellent quality, which was nothing less than she'd expect from him.

She went back down the short corridor to the open-plan living and kitchen area and the tasty aroma of fried vegetables and egg tweaked at her nostrils.

"That smells great," she said, settling onto one of the bar-stools at the granite countertop. "I had no idea you were a cook, as well."

Marcus slid a fluffy omelet from the pan and onto a warmed plate, passing it over to her with a smile. "Oh, I'm a man of many talents."

Avery forked up a mouthful of the omelet and gave a bliss-ful sigh. "That's delicious, thank you."

"You're welcome."

"Where did you learn to cook like that?" she asked as she separated out the individual flavors on her tongue. This was definitely more than your run-of-the-mill bachelor omelet.

Marcus shrugged. "It's nothing special, I did a lot of differ-ent jobs when I was in college. One was working as a kitchen hand." He named one of Boston's top restaurants. "I picked up a few things while I was there."

Avery looked at her plate, stunned to realize she'd already eaten the entire omelet. "Well, they must have been the right few things," she said with a slightly embarrassed laugh.

"Here, have mine," Marcus said, passing his plate, crowned with another perfectly executed omelet, over to her.

"Are you sure?"

"Avery, I'm sure. You know, you ask me that a lot, if I'm sure. I'm the kind of man who doesn't do something unless he is absolutely certain it's the right thing at the time."

"That's good to know," she said, eating the second serv-ing more slowly and watching avidly as Marcus whisked up another mixture.

When Marcus came to sit next to her and eat she asked, "Tell me about tonight. What's the party for?"

"We won the consignment of the notated final-draft man-uscript written by D. B. Dunbar. Have you heard of him?"

"I'm not a great fantasy reader but I know Mrs. Jackson's grandkids are fans. I didn't know there was another manuscript out there. I heard Dunbar was quite young when he died. Wasn't it in a plane crash overseas somewhere?"

"Yeah, in Indonesia. He was only thirty. Too young by any standard. Anyway, the draft is touted to be one of the most valuable pop-culture items currently on the market."

"So Waverly's is celebrating winning the consignment. Is that something you usually do?" Avery asked as she slipped off her stool and took her plate around to the kitchen and rinsed it before putting it in the dishwasher.

"Not usually, no. But I think tonight is a good move on Ann's part. The staff needs a reason to party. We've been in the news a lot lately and not necessarily for good reasons." Marcus's voice was grim.

"Smear campaign?"

"What makes you ask that?" Marcus sat up straighter on his stool, his eyes narrowing as if assessing her.

"I'm not a complete hermit," she said lightly. "I know Waverly's reputation. If I didn't trust the company, let alone you, there is no way on earth you'd be handling Dad's collection. Even I've read the news and there's something about it all that seems a bit forced to me."

"You're right," Marcus said firmly. "Which is why it's even more important that we be seen not to be letting the crap in the papers get to us."

"What time are we expected?"

"Party starts at eight."

Avery flicked a glance at the diamond-studded face of her watch. "I'd say that leaves us a bit of time in hand, wouldn't you?"

Marcus smiled. "Are you thinking what I'm thinking?"

Avery walked back around the counter and reached for his hand, bringing it to her lips and sucking the tip of his index finger softly. "What do you think?"

Eleven

Avery was still bathed in a glow of residual pleasure when they arrived at the party. Marcus was clearly popular with senior and junior staff alike and she couldn't help but notice the avaricious gaze of several of the unattached females alight on him during the course of the evening. He introduced her around as they circulated the room, the crush making the room hot and oppressive.

After a couple of hours, she was grateful when he excused himself to go and speak with one of the newcomers and she took a moment to find an alcove where it was less busy. She was so tired. Maybe it was the air travel or their exertions of the afternoon, or maybe it was just the time difference between London and New York catching up with her but she was pretty much ready to call it a night. If tonight hadn't so obviously been important to Marcus, and to the rest of the Waverly executives and staff, she would have given her apologies and headed back to his apartment.

She went in search of one of the waitstaff circulating with

trays of hors d'oeuvres. Maybe having something to eat would take the edge off her weariness.

"You must be Avery Cullen, how lovely that Marcus brought you along tonight." A tall, willowy blonde reached out a hand to warmly clasp Avery's own. "Ann Richardson, CEO of Waverly's. Marcus has told me a lot about you."

"Including how hard I was to convince about selling the Cullen Collection, I suppose?" Avery answered with a smile.

Despite Ann's cool appearance there was a welcoming twinkle in her blue eyes. "Oh, yes, he might have said something about that. I have to say, Avery, that we are all thrilled to be representing the collection. Your father was well respected in the art world and his taste and acumen were flawless. I was sorry to hear of his passing. You must miss him very much."

Avery felt the familiar sting of loss pierce her chest, but it was not quite as debilitating as before. As if the edges had softened somehow. Was being in love with Marcus the reason why she missed her father a little less now? Or was it because she'd found the courage to let go of the material things that she'd bound Forrest Cullen to her with?

"Yes, I do," she answered simply.

Ann gave her a light touch on the arm, as if in understanding. Anxious to shift the focus of their conversation away from sadness, Avery congratulated Ann on Waverly's latest success.

"Yes, getting the D. B. Dunbar manuscript has been a real coup for us," Ann agreed. "Although it's a shame that *The Last Ninja* will now be his final work."

"He was a schoolteacher, wasn't he? That probably explains why he was so capable of hitting the mark with his audience."

"He taught at a private school in D.C., I believe. And yes, he certainly struck his audience with the right stuff at the right time. There wasn't one that didn't hit the *New York Times* bestseller list."

"Quite an achievement. His family must have been devas

tated about the crash," Avery murmured, referring to the accident that had taken Dunbar's life in October the previous year.

"Not so devastated that it's stopped his only heir, a distant cousin, I believe, from liquidating his entire estate."

"Well, that's good for Waverly's at least," Avery commented drily.

"Indeed. Interest in the auction next month is extremely high already."

Their conversation drifted on to more general topics for a while, before Ann excused herself. Avery watched her walk gracefully away, a part of everything that was going on in the room, yet still holding herself slightly aloof at the same time. Given the negative press the woman had been given Avery had been relieved to find Ann Richardson to be warm and friendly. She found it hard to believe that the rampant rumors of dealing in stolen artifacts had any basis in truth.

Another wave of weariness hit her and Avery looked around for somewhere she could sit while she waited for Marcus, who was still locked in conversation with a group on the other side of the room. As she did so, he looked up and caught her eye. His expression changed swiftly to one of concern and she watched as he left the group and cut through the crowd to be at her side.

"Are you okay? You've gone very pale," he said, hooking an arm around her waist.

She leaned gratefully into his strength. "I don't know what's wrong with me. I'm not usually such a lightweight at parties."

"I'll take you home," he said firmly.

"No, I'll be okay. If necessary I'll take a cab back to your apartment. You can't leave the party already. It's important to you," she protested weakly.

"You're more important."

His words were simple but they hit her with an impact that

brought unexpected tears to her eyes. "Thanks," she said with a watery smile. "Shall we say our goodbyes, then?"

"Let me just tell Ann we're leaving. She can let anyone else know if they're asking. I'll be in the office tomorrow anyway."

It wasn't long before he was back with her and guiding her out to a waiting limousine.

"What's wrong with a cab?" Avery laughed when she saw the car.

"Ann said to use her car, I wasn't about to argue."

They edged across the wide leather seat, Marcus putting his arm around Avery's shoulders and holding her close. She snuggled into his warmth feeling safe, secure, treasured. Marcus had to wake her when they arrived at his building and he solicitously helped her get ready for bed and slide between the decadently smooth cotton sheets before easing his body in behind her. Before she drifted off again, she was aware of his strong arm curled around her waist and the press of his lips against her shoulder.

Marcus was up early the next morning and was surprised to see Avery up and selecting clothes for the day when he exited the bathroom. He was pleased to see she had more color in her face than she had when they'd returned home last night, but there were still shadows beneath her eyes.

"Are you sure you should be up yet?" he asked, reaching for a tie to thread through the crisply pressed collar of his pale blue business shirt.

"Of course. I'll be fine. Besides, if you're going to be at work all day I thought I might spend the day at the Met. There's a gallery talk I'm keen to hear."

"I don't want you overdoing things," he grumbled.

He really meant it. He'd had a nasty surprise when he'd seen how ill, for want of a better word, she'd looked when he'd spied her across the room last night.

"Look, I'll even eat breakfast here before I go if it'll make you feel better," she teased, grabbing her things and slipping past him into the bathroom.

She closed the door behind her and Marcus turned his attention to creating the perfect knot in his tie. He was just about to leave the room when he heard a muffled thump through the bathroom door.

"Avery?" he asked, his hand immediately reaching for the door handle.

No answer.

"Avery!" His voice was louder this time. "Are you okay in there?"

Still nothing. He twisted the knob sharply and pushed open the door, his stomach lurching in fear as he saw her crumpled form collapsed on the tiled floor. He was at her side in an instant, checking her for injury, even as her eyelids began to flutter open.

"Did I faint?" she said, sounding surprised.

"I'll call an ambulance," Marcus said, grabbing for his cell phone in his trouser pocket.

"No, don't do that. I'll be fine. I just got a bit light-headed, is all. Seriously, Marcus. Don't call an ambulance, please," she begged.

"Avery, you're not the kind of person to just faint like that. I insist you at least see a doctor today."

"Don't be silly. Seriously, I'm fine," she said.

He helped her get up, only to feel her sway on her feet. Without another thought he swooped her into his arms and took her through to the bedroom.

"Fine, hmm?" he said, pulling the covers up to her chin. "You'll stay there until I've spoken to a doctor."

It was a measure of how bad she probably felt that Avery didn't argue. Her eyes looked huge in her pale face and he was gripped with an anxiety he was unaccustomed to feeling. He genuinely cared for Avery, perhaps even more than cared for her. Seeing her collapsed on the bathroom floor had been the kind of scare he didn't want to go through again.

He bent to give her a kiss, relieved that her skin was cool to the touch. Sitting down on the bed beside her he scrolled through his cell-phone contact list until he found the number he was looking for. The mother of Daniel Morrison, one of his closest old college friends, had a medical practice right here in Manhattan. Although Marcus knew the practice was closed to new patients, he wasn't above using bribery to get Avery the treatment he demanded, even if it meant relinquishing ownership of the landscape by an acclaimed New Zealand artist that she'd long coveted and which currently resided in pride of place on his office wall at Waverly's.

An hour later they were in a cab and on their way. Avery had eaten a light breakfast in bed, under his supervision, before he'd helped her to the bathroom to bathe and dress. She was cranky as anything by the time they got down to the street but he didn't care. Something was up and they needed to get to the bottom of it.

At the practice they were invited to sit in the tastefully appointed waiting room, a blank wall reminding Marcus of exactly where his friend's mom, Dr. Susanna Morrison, would be hanging the landscape in the next day or two. He shrugged inwardly, it didn't matter. Avery's health was far more important right now. Giving up ownership of the painting had been a small price to pay.

Eventually they were shown through to Susanna's consulting room and Marcus felt Avery relax a little when she realized the doctor was female.

"Hi, Marcus," Susanna said, coming out from behind her desk. "And this must be Avery, pleased to meet you. I'm Susanna Morrison. Now, tell me, what seems to be the problem?"

"Marcus is overreacting. I was a little light-headed this

morning, that's all. It's probably jet lag, we did just fly over from London yesterday," Avery said with a smile.

"I found her unconscious on the bathroom floor. I'm no doctor, but that's a bit more than a little light-headed, I'd say."

"You're right," Susanna agreed, much to his relief. "Have you done this before?"

"No, I generally keep very good health. Life's been a bit up and down lately, that's all. My father died a few months ago and it hit me hard. Maybe it's all just built up?"

Susanna nodded slowly. "Could be, but let's just run a few basic tests before we go any further, okay?" After Avery nodded her assent, the doctor continued. "Would you like Marcus to wait outside while we start?"

Marcus felt himself bristle instantly but conceded that if she was going to have an examination that she'd probably appreciate the privacy. He was surprised, however, when Avery shook her head, her hand creeping into his as if for reassurance.

"No, it's fine, I'm happy for him to stay."

"Okay," the doctor said on an expelled breath and giving Marcus a look with an arched brow.

He met the look squarely. He knew there'd be questions later. He'd never brought the same woman twice to dinner with the Morrison family. It had become a standing joke amongst them. And now, here he was, with a woman in tow and demanding Susanna's medical assistance. Not his usual style, for sure.

"Let's start with your blood pressure," the doctor said, slipping a cuff on Avery's arm. "Hmm," she said after taking the reading. "It's a little on the low side. Do you remember when you had your last period?"

"About a week ago, I had a light bleed. My cycle's been all over the place since Dad died, actually even before that, while he was ill. Lately I've just been really tired, out of routine I expect."

"Okay, let's just do a urine test to rule out a few things."

She showed Avery to a bathroom across the hall from her consulting room. "You'll find everything you need in there. Just take your sample to the nurse's room next door when you're done and she'll do a couple of dip tests and get the results to us immediately."

Marcus fidgeted as the door closed behind Avery and Susanna gave him a hard-edged look. "Care to tell me what this is all about?" she asked in a no-nonsense voice.

"She needs a doctor. You're a doctor, right?"

"Oh, Marcus, this is more than that. I can see the way you look at her. When did you get so serious?"

"It's not…" he started, then stopped abruptly.

He'd been about to deny their relationship emphatically. But he'd suddenly realized it *was* serious. Whatever this thing was between him and Avery, he hadn't had time to examine it thoroughly. Maybe hadn't really wanted to. He'd been a single unit for so long—operating on a mandate of reaching one goal after another in his pursuit of that one elusive success. The chance to pay his Grampa back for his sacrifice twenty-five years ago. Avery had been a means to the end in achieving that goal. When had it all changed so drastically?

"It's complicated," he settled for, finally.

"You're not kidding," Susanna teased him. She patted him on the shoulder. "I can't wait to tell the rest of the family the mighty Marcus has fallen—and fallen hard."

"Yeah, well, don't be in too much of a hurry," he answered, standing up as Avery reentered the room. "You okay?"

"I'm fine, Marcus, really," she said, sitting back down in her chair and squeezing his hand before letting it go. "The tests are just a formality, aren't they?" she asked Susanna.

"They're basic, but I'd like to request a full set of blood tests, too, just in case."

The computer on Susanna's desk pinged a chime and she

gave them both a smile. "That was quick. Looks like our nurse has completed the preliminaries for us."

Marcus felt his stomach knot. "Already?"

"Like I said, these are just preliminary." Susanna fell silent as she scanned the screen. After what felt like an age to Marcus she leaned back in her chair and looked directly at Avery. "It's all looking good. There's no obvious sign of infection or elevated levels of protein in your urine and your glucose seems fine."

"Great, so we can go now?" Avery said, then gave a small laugh. "Not that I don't appreciate you seeing me so promptly and all that but I told Marcus there was nothing to worry about."

"There's certainly nothing medically *wrong* with you—"

"But?" Marcus interrupted. Susanna wasn't giving them the full story and he wanted to know everything, now.

"But your test does appear to show elevated hCG levels," Susanne continued, looking directly at Avery.

"Elevated hCG? Doesn't that mean…" Avery's voice trailed off and she paled again, enough that Marcus put his arm around her just in case she toppled off her chair.

"Mean what?" he demanded.

Susanna looked him square in the eye. "It very likely means that Avery is pregnant."

Twelve

Avery felt a hot flush race through her body. *Pregnant?*

"But that's impossible!" she cried.

"Apparently not. Look, we'll do blood tests to confirm but given your symptoms and the urine-test results I'd say it's the strongest consideration."

Avery faced Marcus who looked every bit as stunned as she felt. "But we used protection. Every single time!"

"Nothing's a hundred-percent effective, except for abstinence, of course. I guess you guys haven't exactly been abstaining?"

"I had a period."

This couldn't be happening to her. It just couldn't.

"I'm guessing that was probably an implantation bleed. Look, I can see this is a shock to you both and clearly there are some decisions you're going to have to make."

"Decisions?" Marcus's voice cut coldly through the fog of shock that had enveloped her body.

"About what you're going to do next. Clearly, if Avery is

pregnant, she's going to have to decide if she wants to continue the pregnancy."

Avery felt as if she had been trapped on an ice floe, floating aimlessly on a dark and dangerous sea. Words failed her. She could barely begin to imagine she was pregnant, let alone consider what came next.

"Anyway," Susanna continued, "we will need proper confirmation so I'll give you the forms for the blood tests and pending those results I'll see you back in a few days, okay?"

She must have responded—good manners were as intrinsic to her as breathing was necessary to life—but she couldn't remember what she'd said. In fact the entire journey back to Marcus's apartment was a blur. Before she knew it they were seated opposite one another, on matching sofas, in his living room.

Marcus looked about as shocked as she felt.

"Are you okay?" she asked, wishing he'd sat beside her rather than so very far away. Right now she could have done with the security of his touch, his warmth.

"I should be asking you that," he replied, his eyes now the murky green of a fathomless lake.

"I'm fine, I guess. A bit shocked." She gave a shaky laugh. "A lot shocked, actually."

"I know. It's a helluva lot to take in."

He fell silent for a while but then his expression changed, as if he'd hit on a solution to a complex puzzle. He rose from his chair and came to her side. She inwardly rejoiced at his nearness, feeling some of her tension ease away just by having him close.

"I've worked it out," he said firmly.

"Worked what out?" What was he talking about? Until they had the tests done and had concrete confirmation there was nothing to work out, surely?

"This—" He gestured toward her, toward her lower belly to be more precise.

Avery had a sudden inkling that she didn't like where this was heading.

"We don't even know for sure that there is a—" she mimicked his gesture "—this!"

But Marcus carried on as if she hadn't spoken. "Marry me, Avery."

Marry him? Avery felt all light-headed again. Not a single word of love had passed his lips and he was suggesting they marry? But even though caution urged her to keep her mouth firmly closed, a tiny part of her, the part that beat solidly for him, ached to say "yes."

"It makes perfect sense," he insisted, holding both her hands and bringing them up to his chest. "Seriously, this is the best solution for us both. Sure, it's old-fashioned, but I think we're both sensible enough to realize that the feelings we have between us can only strengthen. We can make this work, for both our sakes and for that of our child."

When she continued to remain silent he pressed again, "You love me, don't you? Marry me, please?"

It was the unexpected injection of vulnerability in his "please" that was her undoing. And he was right. She did love him. It was a new emotion to her, this type of love. She'd never before felt this level of need for another person the way she did with Marcus. It was terrifying and exhilarating—much as the concept of marriage with him would be.

Marriage.

The word echoed in her mind. It was a major undertaking. A pledge that she knew many didn't take seriously these days but one that she'd always hoped, in her heart of hearts, would be based on a forever love when it happened to her. Could she trust in that belief now, with Marcus? Could they build the kind of marriage that stood the test of decades rather than days?

"Avery? Say something, please?"

He smiled at her, his eyes encouraging her to answer in

the positive, to take a chance. A chance on him and a future together. She wanted to, she really wanted to, but she was so scared. What if it all went wrong? What if he never loved her? What if he came to loathe the very sight of her while she continued to futilely, hopelessly love him?

"I...I don't know, Marcus." She finally gathered the strength to push the words out through her lips. "It's a big step to take. We aren't even sure I'm pregnant, and no matter what, that's no basis for a marriage."

"Marriages have been based on less. C'mon, Avery, you *do* love me, don't you?"

She lifted her eyes to his, to drink in the male beauty of the face she held so dear. "Of course I love you, Marcus. But the question is, do you love me?"

His gaze didn't falter. "I care about you deeply, Avery. More than I've ever cared for another person in my life aside from my Grampa. Honestly. I truly think we can make it work."

"And if I'm not pregnant?"

"Then we'll still be married. C'mon, let's do it," he urged. "We can get a license and be married straightaway."

"You make it all sound so easy."

"It is easy, Avery."

"Let me think about it, okay?" she implored him. "I don't want to rush into something this important."

"Okay," Marcus conceded. "Is the rest of today long enough?"

She laughed incredulously. "Marcus! That's hardly fair. You're suggesting something that is supposed to last our lifetimes and you want me to make my mind up just like that?"

"I made my mind up about you in a lot less time," he said, leaning forward to press a kiss upon her slightly parted lips.

Instant heat, instant desire. Even through all the fear and confusion of this morning he had this power over her. She could have this forever if she was only brave enough to say "yes."

Marcus interrupted her thoughts. "I need to get into the office for a few hours today. I tell you what, you stay here and rest, I'll take you out somewhere wonderful for dinner tonight and we'll talk about it more then."

"Surely I'll be okay at the Met. I'm feeling much stronger now—and I'll have some lunch before I go."

"I'll take you another time, I promise, just humor me for today." He reached out a hand to smooth a lock of hair from her cheek. "You scared me this morning. I didn't know how to deal with you when I didn't know what was wrong. Now we know that you might be pregnant, that's something we can handle—together. But I still want to know you're safe. Please, for me, just rest today, okay?"

His care for her was obvious in every syllable of every word he spoke. Was it enough, though? Could they build a future on that?

"Okay," she answered huskily, "but only if you *promise* you'll take me to the Met another day."

"I said I would, didn't I? So, it's a deal," he said. "I won't let you down, Avery. Ever."

She clung to his words after he'd gone, wanting to believe them. Suddenly ravenously hungry, she made herself a sandwich and a bowl of fruit salad and took them both over to the sofa where she ate her way through her food and thought. And thought some more.

Marcus hadn't lied to her about his feelings. He hadn't suddenly filled her ears with protestations of love everlasting. If he had she probably wouldn't have believed him anyway. He had, however, been honest and that had a great deal to be said about it.

He cared about her. Was that enough? Deep down she knew she wanted his eternal love—caring was just the beginning, wasn't it? At least, if she agreed to his harebrained scheme, they had a strong starting point. For centuries, marriages the world round had begun with less and thrived and been successful.

She didn't *need* to marry him. She had more than enough money not to ever be dependant on another soul the rest of her life. But money wasn't love. It could keep you comfortable, feed you physically—but nothing but love fed your soul. Avery flicked a glance at the clock on the microwave oven in the kitchen. Midday. She sighed. It was going to be a very long afternoon.

Marcus went through the motions at the office. He'd been away long enough that there was a pile of paperwork to sort through, even though the redoubtable Lynette had certainly made a big dent in it for him. A confirmation from the shipping company in L.A. told him that the Cullen collection would be arriving over the weekend. Marcus made a silent vow to be there when the collection was inventoried and accepted into the system. He couldn't wait to see it with his own eyes.

Already the thrill of putting together the auction catalog rushed through his veins. The proofs had come through from the photographer and Lynette had already earmarked those she felt should be used in advance publicity for the auction.

There still remained one black spot on his happy horizon. *Lovely Woman.*

A new thought came crashing down upon him. If Avery agreed to marry him then the painting would surely become part of their matrimonial property. One way or another, it would be his, even if jointly. There was only one stumbling block to this new and exhilarating idea, and that was if she refused to marry him.

He pushed his chair back from his desk and swiveled around until he faced the window. He didn't even bother to stare down at the view of Madison Avenue and its bustling street life. Instead he propped his elbows on his knees and rested his head in his hands. How had this all gotten so out of control? He reexamined the way the past few weeks had panned out and he could see no other route than the one he'd taken.

Marriage. It was a monumentally big step. His grandfather would kill him if he had the slightest inkling that Marcus didn't love Avery the way a man marrying a woman should love her. But for the chance to be reunited with the painting that was rightfully theirs? The painting that had almost destroyed his great-grandmother's livelihood and had put unmentionably unfair financial strain upon her young shoulders?

Avery had to agree to his proposal. She just had to.

He sat upright and swiveled his chair back around. He had to work on the assumption she'd agree—anything else was incomprehensible—and that meant he needed to be prepared.

"Lynette?" he called.

His PA appeared in his doorway as if she'd been awaiting his summons. The woman must move with the speed of greased lightning, but he was grateful for that right now.

"Yes, Mr. Price?"

It still felt odd that a woman old enough to be his mother referred to him so formally while he called her by her first name. But, despite him having requested otherwise several times, she refused to budge.

"I'd like you to research something for me."

"Of course, Mr. Price. What is it exactly?"

To her credit she didn't so much as blink when he gave her his answer. "A marriage license—for this weekend."

"Certainly, it won't take me a moment."

And it didn't. To his delight she presented him with all the information he needed to make their wedding ceremony happen. All he needed now was to complete the paperwork, pay the fee—and for Avery to say yes.

Later in the afternoon Marcus made reservations for dinner at his favorite restaurant in the Theater District. The ambience, the food, the service—it would all be perfect. It was good to know there were some things he could guarantee and he liked being prepared ahead of time.

It was his attention to detail that drove him out of the office and toward one of the jewelers who specialized in antique reproductions. He didn't think Avery was the type to go for a modern-day ice rink on her finger. Everything about her was subtle, understated, yet elegant and beautiful at the same time. Finding the right ring to seal their agreement was all-important. He didn't even want to speculate that she might not agree.

He knew he'd found the right ring when his attention was drawn to a blue and white diamond ring set in platinum.

"How may we help you, sir?" a dark-suited older gentleman asked as Marcus peered into the display case.

"This ring," he said, pointing. "I'd like a closer look."

"You have excellent taste, sir," the clerk remarked as he disabled the alarm on the case and unlocked it to remove the ring in question. "Elegance and exceptional quality combined."

He elaborated on the blue diamond's attributes, including its pure and unenhanced color, but Marcus could only think of how much it reminded him of the blue of Avery's eyes when they made love. It was perfect. The central round stone at just over two carats certainly managed to catch and disperse the overhead lighting to great effect. Its flanking pair of brilliant-cut white diamonds were also set to great advantage in the intricately engraved band while smaller white diamonds glittered in the shoulders on either side.

"This is a 1920s reproduction, and the craftsmanship is quite exquisite, wouldn't you say?" The clerk wound up his sales babble.

"Is there a wedding band to match?"

"Certainly, sir."

The clerk unlocked a drawer beneath the display case and removed a band from the cushioned tray. He held it out to Marcus for his perusal. Set in the same style as the shoulders of the engagement ring, the band sparkled with small white diamonds while the sides also bore the intricate engraving featured on the other ring.

"Great, I'll take them both," Marcus said decisively.

"I'm sure your fiancée will be delighted."

I sure hope so, Marcus thought privately. The cost of the ring was a small price to pay if it helped to convince Avery he was serious about his proposal.

Avery met him at the door to the apartment when he got home. He'd barely extracted his key from the lock and shut the door behind him when she pressed herself up against him, wrapped her arms around his neck and kissed him full hard on the lips.

"I could get used to being welcomed home like that," he said, dipping his head to capture her lips again. When he drew back he asked, "Have you reached a decision?"

"Yes," she said softly.

Marcus felt his heart leap in his chest but he forced himself to disentangle from her embrace and take a small step back. "Just so I'm completely clear, yes, you've made a decision, or, yes, you're accepting my proposal?"

She smiled back at him and she'd never looked so beautiful. She nodded. "Yes, I'm accepting your proposal. I've been thinking about it all afternoon and you're right. We can make this work, I know it."

Marcus gave a whoop of delight, not realizing until this moment how tense he'd been as he awaited her decision. He picked her up and whirled her around in his arms.

"You won't regret it," he said, setting her back down on her feet again.

Grasping her by the hand, he led her over to the sofa and sat her down, before kneeling on the floor at her feet. He reached into his pocket and took out the jeweler's box containing her engagement ring. Opening it so it faced her, he said, "Let's do this properly. Avery Cullen, will you do me the honor of becoming my wife?"

"Oh, Marcus, you didn't have to do this," she said shakily. "But it *is* beautiful."

"Waiting for an answer here," he teased with a smile, feeling untold relief now that everything was falling into place.

"Yes," she breathed. "Yes, I will."

He extracted the ring from its satin bed and slid it on her finger, pushing it firmly over her knuckle. The action was as old-fashioned as time, as overplayed as a scenario possibly could be—and yet it felt so incredibly right.

"I hope you're a fan of short engagements," Marcus said, rising to sit on the sofa next to her.

"How short were you thinking?"

"This weekend?"

"This weekend! Are you serious?"

"Never more so. What's the point in waiting? We've made our decision."

She drew in a deep breath and looked him square in the eye. "You're right," she said. "We have. But seriously, can we get married so soon? Aren't there waiting times and restrictions?"

"Lynette looked into it for me today. If we apply for the license tomorrow we have a twenty-four-hour waiting period so there's nothing to stop us marrying on Sunday."

"Where will we marry?"

"That probably depends on who I can get to officiate at this notice. Is that a problem?"

"No," she said slowly. "But if you don't mind, I'd like to ask one of my father's oldest friends if he'd officiate for us."

"He's a celebrant?"

"You could say that. He's a New York State Supreme Court judge."

"But that's great! He can waive the waiting period for us. We can marry on Saturday, instead." Marcus pulled his cell phone from his pocket. "Call him now, see if he's willing."

They were in luck; Judge Harwood was free and more than willing to preside over the wedding of his old friend's only daughter. He had one proviso; that Avery be married at his home. It meant she wouldn't be with Marcus on Friday night as the judge's wife had suggested she stay with them at their house the night before the wedding, but that was a small sacrifice to pay. After Saturday, Avery would be with him every night—and he couldn't wait.

By the time Saturday afternoon rolled along Marcus was as fidgety as a cat on a hot-tin roof. Avery's pregnancy had been confirmed yesterday, which had put a whole new perspective on everything in Marcus's eyes.

This was for real. His own parents had never married—nor had they ever cared about the child they'd conceived. To his father he'd been no more than a bargaining chip for more money. Marcus had never planned to have children, certainly not before he was even thirty. But he was about to become a father, with all that entailed, and he was going to do right by his child and his child's mother. No matter how daunting that would be.

He readjusted the cuffs on his shirt for the third time in ten minutes. It wasn't that he was nervous exactly, although he had to admit to a moment's concern when faced with the gimlet eye of Judge Seymour Harwood for the first time about half an hour ago. The man's handshake had been firm to the point of being vicelike and Marcus hadn't mistaken the underlying warning in Judge Harwood's tone when he'd said he hoped Marcus would take good care of Avery.

Now, standing on the edge of the garden and waiting for Avery to come out of the house he felt as if the eyes of the few friends who had been able to attend at such short notice were drilling holes into him. No one more so than Macy Tarlington who sat in the front row with her cowboy.

He and Avery had both eschewed attendants, given that they'd organized the wedding so quickly, but Marcus kind of wished now that he had someone at his side. A flash of guilt seared him momentarily. He should have told his grandfather of his plans, but it had seemed easier to avoid the piercing questions he knew would come his way when Grampa heard of the news. He wasn't ready to face those just yet.

The string quartet that had been playing quietly in the background suddenly broke off, only to resume with the opening strains of the wedding march. Marcus felt as if his tie had suddenly become inextricably tight as he turned and faced his bride.

She was a vision. There was no other way to describe her. The rays of the late-afternoon sun gilded Avery's skin with a gentle touch, emphasizing her radiant glow as her eyes met his—the distance between them closing in an instant. And in that moment Marcus knew he was irrevocably lost. This was no marriage for the sake of a baby. It was no marriage so he could finally, finally, recover his family's lost treasure.

It was a marriage based on love—Avery's, and his—and the realization almost paralyzed him with fear.

Thirteen

As honeymoons went the night of their wedding was all too short. He'd make it up to her in the next few weeks, Marcus thought as he lay awake in the dawn with Avery curled within the protective circle of his arms. He would. Right now he was still coming to terms with the weight of the discovery that he was in love with his wife. He'd never given love much thought before. This, however, was something he had to think about and face and learn to deal with. And he had no idea how.

Everything in Marcus's life, from the time he could make his own decisions, had been quantifiable. Every step he'd taken on the road of his life since he'd been a studious young boy with a dream in his heart had been deliberate. He knew where he was going, what he wanted and why. But this, this overwhelming emotion people called love, was different. It was nothing like the deep affection that existed between him and his grandfather—an affection that had developed over years with the balance of care and responsibility shifting from one to the other with time and age. This was passion and intensity and a gut-gripping anxiety all rolled into one.

Caring about Avery had been safe. Loving her was terrifying. He didn't trust it. Couldn't. Even as they'd made love last night, the actions weighted now with far more than the giving and receiving of pleasure, he hadn't been able to share his newly discovered feelings for her in words. Giving her that power over him, admitting it, went against everything Marcus knew.

He could barely remember exchanging vows with her yesterday but he had a vivid picture in his mind as the solemnity of the promises they'd exchanged hit home while he'd eased her wedding ring on her finger. He lifted her hand now, looking at the ring that evidenced the bond forged between them. He hadn't even given that bond a thought when he'd chosen it. He'd been so stupidly naive.

When he'd asked her to marry him he'd said he cared for her. *Cared for her!* God, what had he been thinking? This feeling, this overwhelming need for her and to protect her, it had been there right from the start. She was the one. His one. How had he never seen that?

He knew how. He'd been so focused on getting her to agree to sell, and on getting his hands on *Lovely Woman* he'd ignored what his heart was telling him about the lovely woman in his arms.

Thinking about it sent his mind spinning in circles, forcing him to ask questions of himself and examine those answers with an honesty he wasn't ready for. Didn't know if he'd ever be ready for. So, for now he'd hold his feelings for his wife deep inside, where they could do no harm. To her, or to him.

Marcus pried himself from Avery's embrace, despite her sleepy protests. Married or not, weekend or not, he had work scheduled for today. The Cullen Collection was supposed to have arrived overnight and he had promised Avery he'd be there to oversee it being unpacked.

Three quarters of an hour later he was occupied with the time-consuming task of supervising the uncrating and cross-checking the inventory list of the collection. Time passed quickly and he was on the verge of directing the staff to take a break when his cell phone rang.

He checked the caller ID and, not recognizing the number let the call go to voice mail. Clearly the caller wasn't satisfied with that because less than a minute later the phone started up again.

"Hey, guys, why don't you head out for some lunch and meet back here in about an hour, okay?" Marcus directed. It was time they all had some air, anyway.

As the two men who'd been assisting him left the storeroom he accepted the call with a clipped greeting.

"Dalton Rothschild here, I'm glad you could take my call."

Marcus looked around to make sure the staff had left and closed the door to the storeroom. He didn't want anyone eavesdropping on a conversation with the head of Waverly's biggest competitor. It was too easy for a few casually overheard words to be misconstrued. Although why Rothschild wanted to speak with him had him burning with curiosity.

"To what do I owe the pleasure?" he asked, injecting just the right note of insolence. To be perfectly frank, despite Rothschild's handsome and urbane exterior, Marcus thought the man was a snake and he knew Rothschild wasn't above manipulating other people for his own ends. The planting of one of his assistants as a spy within Waverly's being a perfect case in point.

"I have a proposition to put to you, Price. Meet me for dinner so we can discuss it."

Marcus allowed himself a grim smile. Hardly an invitation. More like a summons. But there was something about the word *proposition* that intrigued him. What the hell was the man up to now? Marcus had no doubt Ann would be equally as fascinated to find out. Maybe this time they'd catch the latest rumor early, giving them a chance to refute it before it could blow up in their faces. He didn't want to sound too eager, though.

"Mr. Rothschild, I'm sure you know the ramifications if I'm seen dining with you. The rumor mill will work overtime, especially given the current trend of useless speculation about Waverly's." Speculation Marcus believed Rothschild had been feeding to the media like kindling on a fire. After all, as Waverly's key opposition, Rothschild stood to gain the most if Waverly's went to the wall.

"Which is precisely why we need to meet. Six o'clock, tomorrow evening, Price. At my apartment since you're so determined on privacy." He rattled off his address and hung up before Marcus had time to react.

Avery was none too happy to be left to her own devices for the second day in a row after her marriage. *Second day? Second night, more like,* she thought as she faced another long evening alone. She'd been asleep when Marcus had come home from Waverly's last night and then this morning, Monday, he'd left early for the office again. His kiss had been perfunctory at best when he'd said goodbye. She understood he had to make up for the time he'd recently spent in London with her, but his air of distraction, as if he was occupied by something far more important to him than his new wife, had her worried.

And she knew exactly what that something was. The Cullen Collection. Just thinking about it made her stomach lurch. Had this been what he'd wanted all along? Why had she never questioned what lengths he'd been prepared to go to procure the paintings for sale? Had he even been prepared to go so far as to marry her? No, now she was being ridiculous. She'd

already agreed to let Marcus represent the collection long before he'd proposed to her. Long before they'd discovered they
were about to become parents.

She pressed a palm to her belly. Was that what it was, then?
Was he regretting she was pregnant? Did he regret marrying
her? They'd been husband and wife for all of two days and
aside from their time in bed, he'd spent scant minutes with
her awake. They'd rushed into this, she knew, but she'd been
so certain in her heart of hearts that she'd made the right decision. Had she been totally naive and gullible all over again?
Was this a repeat of the pattern that had plagued her all her
life when it came to friends and relationships?

He didn't strike her as the kind of man who just wanted
her for her fortune. She'd learned, the hard way, to recog-
nize those types. No, Marcus's hot button was definitely art
and he had already achieved what he wanted to with her father's paintings.

All except *Lovely Woman*.

A chill ran down her back, radiating out to immobilize
her whole body in its frozen grip. Was that what it was? One
painting? Had he married her just to get hold of that one painting? Avery tried to push the thought from her mind, telling
herself it was stupid but in her mind's eye she could still see
Marcus's face when he'd seen the canvas for the first time.
He'd wanted it, bad.

The phone rang, and she was thankful for the interruption
because she didn't want to pursue those thoughts. They had
to be too ridiculous to give credence to.

"How's my favorite wife?" The sound of Marcus's voice
chased away her fears. He was real, he had feelings for her,
she knew it. It was there in his tone and in the way he made
love to her. She tried to grab on to that thought but, for some
reason, it slipped through her metaphorical fingertips.

"Last time I checked I was your only wife, or are you holding out on me?"

Despite her best efforts there was a note in her voice that bordered on unease.

"Are you okay, Avery?"

She closed her eyes and squeezed the handset of the phone tight, forcing herself to draw in a steadying breath before she spoke again.

"Of course I'm okay. Just missing you, that's all."

She heard him sigh on the other end of the line. "I'm sorry but you're going to have to miss me a bit more. I have to work late. I'd rather be home with you but it's unavoidable."

Avery caught her lower lip between her teeth and bit hard. She wasn't going to beg him to come home. She wasn't.

"Oh? That's a shame. When can I expect you, then?"

"I'm not sure. Look, don't wait up, but promise me you'll eat. Order something, okay?"

"Don't worry, I'll take care of myself. I'm used to it."

"Avery, don't be like that," he said quietly.

"Like what? I am used to looking after myself, Marcus. Seriously, don't worry about me."

"I'll be home as soon as I can."

"I look forward to it."

She disconnected the call and wandered over to the large window that looked out at the view and suddenly felt overwhelmingly homesick for her garden in Kensington. Her father would be proud of the garden were he still alive. But would he be proud of her, too? She wrapped her arms around her middle and held herself tight and, despite the little person she knew was growing within her, she felt more alone than she ever had in her life.

Avery jumped when her cell phone rang. Her heart raced, hope building in her chest that it was Marcus calling to say he'd changed his plans and would be home after all.

"Hello?" She sounded breathless, needy, but she didn't care. If it was Marcus she just wanted him here.

"Avery? Is that you?"

Hope dashed into a million tiny fragments at her feet. She recognized the man's voice, and it certainly wasn't her husband.

"Peter. I didn't expect to hear from you again. How did you find me?"

"I heard through the grapevine that you and Marcus Price got married last weekend. Is that right?"

"That's right," she answered cautiously. It hadn't taken long for news to travel but it didn't explain why he was calling her.

"Look, there are some things you really should know. Things I don't want to disclose over the phone. I'm in New York for meetings with the boss but I'm free tonight. Can you get away, maybe meet me somewhere?"

Avery's initial instinct was to bristle and refuse Peter Cameron's request point blank. What could he possibly have to tell her that was worse than what he'd tried to put her off Marcus with back in London? Caution made her hold her tongue. Caution and her own fears about why Marcus had married her.

"I might be able to manage that, where were you thinking of meeting?"

He named an Italian restaurant only a couple of blocks from the apartment.

"Okay. I'll see you there in an hour."

"Thanks, you won't regret it."

She had a suspicion that she'd regret it deeply, but her own fears drove her to change into a pair of dark trousers and boots and to throw on her warm coat to ward off the evening chill as she walked to the restaurant.

Peter was already seated at a booth when she arrived. She eased herself onto the bench seat opposite him.

"I thought we could order first, then talk," Peter said, passing her one of the two menus on the table.

Remembering her promise to Marcus, Avery scanned the menu and made her selection, requesting sparkling mineral water with her meal. Thankfully their meals arrived promptly, negating the need to make small talk.

As Avery lifted the first forkful of carbonara to her mouth, Peter began to talk.

"So, congratulations on your marriage," he started. "But maybe I should be congratulating Marcus instead."

"Why not congratulate us both?" Avery asked, confused.

"I kind of think he'll be getting more out this than you imagine."

"How so?" she demanded, putting her fork down on her plate. This had been a bad move. She should never have come.

"Well, you remember me telling you about his parents?"

"Yes, but I don't see what that has to do with anything. Marcus is who he is and he's worked hard to get *where* he is."

Peter gave her a sly look. "Did he work hard on you?"

Avery started to rise from her seat. "I don't need to listen to this."

"Please, sit down. It's important."

She hesitated a moment before settling back down. "Get to the point."

"Aren't you going to eat?" he asked, gesturing to her plate.

"Actually, I've lost my appetite. What do you mean Marcus will get more out of our marriage than I imagine?"

He shrugged and swirled up more of his spaghetti, taking his time chewing and swallowing before speaking again.

"You didn't get him to sign a prenuptial agreement, did you?"

Of course she didn't. She loved him. She believed their marriage would work, or at least she *had* believed that. Her silence prompted Peter to continue.

"He must be pretty thrilled to be a joint owner now of *Lovely Woman*. It is what he wanted all along. Did you know that?"

A fist clenched tight in her chest. "Stop beating around the bush, Peter, or I'm leaving now."

"No, you're not. You want to hear this probably about as much as I want to tell it to you." He gave her a half smile. "As I said before, you know what happened to Marcus's parents and how his grandfather raised him."

"Yes, I know all that."

"You might be interested to know that his grandfather's mother was Kathleen Price—née O'Reilly." At Avery's blank look he kept going. "If my sources are correct, Kathleen O'Reilly was the model in *Lovely Woman* and, if I'm not mistaken, your great-great-uncle's lover. How's that for a coincidence? But you see, it gets more interesting. Apparently one of Baxter Cullen's old notebooks, on loan to The Old State House museum in Boston, shows that the painting was gifted to someone with the initials K.O. I'd say that someone could only be Kathleen O'Reilly, who then left it to her only son when she passed away. Quite a legacy, wouldn't you say—a Baxter Cullen original?

"But clearly not enough of a legacy for her son, because twenty-five years ago he sold the painting, and your father had the good sense to buy it. Marcus approached your father several times to buy it back before he died. Did you know that?"

Avery felt her face pale, felt hope drain from her to be replaced by a sickening numbness. She shook her head in response to Peter's question, not that he needed one, because he continued to spread his poison.

"You've got to hand it to him for ingenuity. A whirlwind romance and sudden marriage, so romantic—until you look at his motivation. In marrying you, Marcus has finally found a way to get the painting back. Rather clever, don't you think?"

Clever was definitely not the first word that came to mind. In fact, no words came to mind. Only a long, painful, silent howl of pain from deep, deep inside. There was a chance Peter was lying, but she doubted it. Everything fit together too well and it wasn't as if he had anything to gain by telling her.

She'd thought Marcus was different but he'd used her just like everyone else had, except his betrayal was the worst of all.

Marcus arrived at Dalton Rothschild's apartment building, surprised to be greeted by name by the concierge. Still, he supposed, nothing about Dalton Rothschild ought to surprise him. When talk of collusion between Ann Richardson and Rothschild had been bandied about last month, after Ann had been rumored in the media to be romantically linked with the man, Marcus had no doubt where those rumors had originated. Rothschild was not the kind of man who would take being publicly dumped lying down. He was, however, the kind of man who would seek revenge.

Was this another of Rothschild's attempts to undermine Waverly's? Even though the talk of collusion had included his name as much as it had Ann's, he'd still managed to come out of everything smelling like roses—while Ann continued to be pilloried by an unforgiving media. Did Rothschild plan to try wooing away senior executives and staff to weaken Waverly's position even further?

In their industry, reputation counted for a lot, and Ann, the board and the rest of the staff were all committed to protecting what was left of Waverly's. Loyalty was everything right now.

The journey up in the elevator was smooth and swift, not unlike Rothschild himself, Marcus thought privately. A neatly suited man waited for him as the doors opened on Rothschild's floor.

"Good evening, Mr. Price. I'm Sloane, Mr. Rothschild's assistant. If you'd come with me?"

Marcus followed him down the thickly carpeted corridor to a set of double doors at the end. Sloane keyed in a code, then pressed his thumb against a scanner. Marcus was impressed with the security and he understood why it was necessary as they entered the foyer of the apartment. Priceless antiques were everywhere—from the richly jewel-toned carpet on the floor to the light fixtures hanging from the ceiling. It was like walking into a museum. A very tastefully furnished museum that was lived in. Marcus briefly admired a cloisonné enamel plaque on the wall. If he wasn't mistaken, it dated back to the twelfth century. He'd only ever seen pictures of one before but this was something else.

"Beautiful, isn't it?" Rothschild's voice interrupted Marcus's assessment of the piece.

"Indeed," Marcus agreed, shaking the hand offered.

"Thank you, Sloane, I'll look after Mr. Price from here." Rothschild dismissed his assistant and gestured to Marcus to follow him through to the sitting room. "Drink?" he asked, moving toward a sideboard.

"Thanks, whiskey, straight up."

"Hard day at the office?" Rothschild asked, a sly smile pulling at his lips.

As if he'd admit to that. "No more than usual."

"I hear congratulations are in order," his host continued after pouring two whiskeys and handing one to Marcus.

"Congratulations?"

"On your marriage and on acquiring the Cullen Collection."

"News travels fast," Marcus said noncommittally.

"Oh, yes, if one cares to listen. Tell me, was marrying Avery Cullen part of the deal?"

Anger clawed at Marcus's throat, demanding he tell Dalton Rothschild exactly what he thought of his offensive remark, but reason prevailed. He wanted to find out why he'd been summoned here, so he could report back to Ann in the morning. She'd been surprised when Marcus had told her of the invitation, and just as curious as he was as to Rothschild's intent.

"With all due respect, my marriage is none of your concern," he answered stiffly.

The other man just smiled, a calculating expression in his eyes. "I like you, Price. It's not every man who's prepared to go above and beyond the call of duty like that."

Marcus refused to be goaded into a response, instead taking a sip of the fine single malt liquor and allowing himself a moment to appreciate it. He was surprised when Rothschild changed his conversational tack, and began to prove himself to be a consummate host. Under other circumstances, Marcus could almost have enjoyed himself. In fact, it was easy to see how Ann may have been drawn into this particular spider's web. But at the back of his mind was the fact that his host never appeared to do anything without an ulterior motive, and while Marcus's every instinct urged him to go home to his wife, where he belonged, he owed it to Ann to find out what that motive was.

It wasn't until they were at the ornately set dining table and enjoying a particularly fine glass of merlot with their meal that Rothschild finally got to the point of their meeting.

"I'll stop beating around the bush, Price. I admire your work ethic. Your results with Waverly's have been nothing short of outstanding. You're wasted there. That particular house of cards is not far from falling and when it does fall, it's not going to be pretty. I'd hate to see you caught up in the debris. I want you to come and work for me." Rothschild named a key position and a salary that just about made Marcus's teeth ache. "And I want you to bring the Cullen Collection with you."

Rothschild certainly knew how to make an offer appealing, Marcus thought. If he'd been raised with less scruples than he had, he'd have jumped at the offer.

"That's a very generous offer," Marcus conceded, not being drawn into giving a more definite response.

"But?"

"But I won't accept."

"You won't? Come now, Marcus—I can call you Marcus, can't I?" Rothschild asked with a smile, directing the full force of his charisma toward his guest. "You're an intelligent man, and an astute one. Do you really wish to see your hard-fought-for reputation sullied by working for Ann Richardson?

"I know how hard you worked to get where you are today—it's not every kid from your background who manages to break free of the mold and achieve what you have so far. With the right support, who knows where you might be in another ten years? Maybe even in my chair at Rothschild's." He gave an elegant shrug.

"I'm flattered you researched me so thoroughly," Marcus replied with a smile that gave no clue to the fury that remained on a slow boil inside him.

"Oh, I'm a very thorough man, Marcus. Which is why I'm surprised you've tagged your allegiance to someone like Ann Richardson. She's dealing in stolen artifacts, you know that, don't you? It won't be long before she's exposed for the fraud she truly is. And let's not forget the matter of trying to get me to collude with her earlier. She's a nasty piece of work. When she falls, and she will, everyone at Waverly's, from the top down, will be tarred with the same brush."

Marcus's fingers tightened on the delicate stem of the Waterford crystal goblet in his hand. He deliberately put the glass back down on the table before he broke it, but only out of respect for the craftsmanship of the maker, not its owner. It was sickening hearing the lengths Rothschild was prepared to go to in his quest to destroy his rival.

Ann Richardson was in no way capable of the duplicity that his host had accused her of; Marcus knew that to the depths of his soul. The woman had integrity and she had believed in Marcus from the very start of his career with Waverly's. It was that belief in him that had given him the impetus he needed to move through the ranks in the company faster than even he'd anticipated. Her actions, her support, her encouragement—none of it had been the action of a duplicitous person.

In many ways Ann had reminded Marcus of his grandfather. Honorable to a fault and prepared to stand by those she believed in, she'd employed him fresh from college. Ann had actively encouraged his more ambitious ideas, while using judiciously given guidance at the same time. He owed a lot to her, including his unswerving loyalty.

"You present a passionate argument, Mr. Rothschild," Marcus said, holding on to civility by a thread. "However you have forgotten one very important aspect."

"Oh, really? And what might that be?"

Marcus was pleased to see his comment had wiped some of the smugness off the man's handsome face.

"The truth," he said bluntly. "Thank you for this evening, it's been most enlightening, and thank you for your offer, which I refuse." He rose from the table, pushing his chair back on the highly polished floor with a loud scrape. "Don't worry about seeing me out, I can find my own way."

Avery jumped up from the sofa when she heard Marcus's key in the lock. Her legs trembled beneath her as she stood waiting for him to come in. In the two hours since she'd left Peter Cameron's loathsome company she had a lot of time to think, and the thinking had brought her to a decision.

People had used her for her money and her contacts ever since she'd been in kindergarten. She should have seen this coming. She was absolutely the worst kind of fool to have been taken in by some slick Bostonian fraud. As she'd fought

through the numbed shock Peter's revelations had wrought
she'd begun to wonder if everyone at Waverly's wasn't like
Marcus. After all, there had been a great deal of negative
publicity about them so far. Maybe there was an element of
truth to it after all.

It was too late to withdraw her assignation of the sale
rights of her father's artworks, and the knowledge made her
feel slightly ill. She'd been thoroughly duped—more the fool
herself. What was that old saying? Fool me once, shame on
you—fool me twice, shame on me? Well the shame was hers
to bear, and bear it she would. But not here. Not with Marcus. And, if she had her way, she'd never have to see him
again after tonight.

She heard Marcus come in through the door and she waited
for his reaction when he saw the luggage she had waiting in
the foyer.

"What the— Avery, what's going on?"

She fought the twist of her heart as she saw him when he
came into the room, his face a mixture of anger and confusion.

"I'm leaving."

"What? But why?"

Was he so confident of himself, of his appeal to her, that it
had never crossed his mind that she might find out his lies?
Her eyes burned with the sting of unshed tears and she looked
up to the ceiling for a moment in an attempt to halt their fall.

"I should have thought the why would be obvious to someone as astute as you."

His face hardened. "I don't know what you're talking
about."

"Tell me, Marcus, why did you really come to London?"

"It was never a secret. You know I came to persuade you
to agree to sell your father's collection. I'd tried through the
usual routes, which you very effectively blocked, so I ap-

roached you directly. I don't get it. I thought you were happy with your decision. Are you saying you want to withdraw rom the sale?"

"And would that matter to you?" she asked.

"Of course it would matter, but if that's what you really wanted then that's what would happen. I only want you to be happy."

He reached out to take her hands in his but Avery took a step back.

"Don't. Don't touch me."

Marcus reacted as if she'd slapped him. "Tell me, Avery. What's wrong? What's upset you so much?"

She drew in a leveling breath, determined to see this through. It would be so easy to give in, to tell him she was just being irrationally moody. Every cell, every nerve in her body begged her to do that—to close the yawning distance between them and to press her body against his, to take from him what he had so readily given her. But her head and her heart urged caution, because while he'd given freely of his body, he had withheld the truth.

"Do you remember when I went to that gallery opening in London, and I came home early?"

"Of course I do. You were upset."

"Did you ever wonder why?"

He huffed a sigh of impatience. "Of course I wondered why, but I figured it was your business and if you wanted me to know about it, you'd tell me."

Avery suddenly wished she had. Maybe it would have given him an opening, a chance to come clean with the truth rather than her forcing it from him now.

"I bumped into a mutual acquaintance, Peter Cameron, that night."

Marcus face twisted in a scowl. "He's no acquaintance of mine."

"Well, for someone who isn't even an acquaintance of yours, he seemed to know an awful lot about you. Things he felt it was important for me to know, too."

"Is that right? What sort of things?" Marcus shoved his hands in his pockets and rocked back on his heels as if telling her that no matter what she had to say, it couldn't hurt him. His body language intimating he was as open as he could be.

"Things about your background. Your parents."

"So he told you my mother was a junkie who died in jail and my father was the no-good drug pusher who made that all happen?" His face remained expressionless, but he wasn't able to hide the dark pain in his eyes. "I was a baby when that happened. My past is not who *I* am."

"I know that!" she snapped. "What he told me then didn't matter. It just showed me how determined you were to succeed *despite* everything. He actually did you a service. He helped me to understand why you are so driven to be the best, why doing well is so important to you."

"So why are you leaving me if I'm apparently such a paragon?" A note of bitterness colored his voice.

"Because he asked to meet me tonight."

"And you went? After he upset you so much the last time? Why?"

"Why isn't really important."

"Like hell it isn't! Tell me, Avery. Why did you go when you knew he would only have more crap to dish out?"

She swallowed against the lump that had built in her throat. "He had something to tell me. Something you probably should have told me when we met, to be honest. It might have made a difference."

"Something I should have told you?" Marcus looked confused. "Like what? Do I get a chance to refute what he said? A chance to give you the truth, which I seriously doubt you heard from the likes of Peter Cameron."

"Tell me now, then. Tell me *who* you are," Avery demanded. "Tell me exactly who you are—going back, oh, let's say, three generations."

She saw the moment he realized she knew the truth.

"Lovely Woman."

"So you don't refute what Peter said?"

"Of course I don't. I can't deny the truth."

She had thought she couldn't hurt any more than she had up to this moment. But she'd been wrong. She gave a bitter laugh. "Although you want to, don't you? You know, if you'd been honest with me from the start I might have considered selling her to you, for the *right* reasons. But now?" She gave a sharp shake of her head. "You can forget ever so much as seeing the painting again. You lied to me all along, about why you wanted to represent Dad's collection, about why you wanted *Lovely Woman* included. When have you ever been a hundred percent truthful with me, Marcus? When?"

The silence between them stretched out uncomfortably. Unable to stand it any longer Avery bent and picked up her handbag from the sofa.

"Thanks for at least not lying to me now. You know, I don't know why I didn't see it sooner. Owning *Lovely Woman* was all that mattered to you, wasn't it? I was merely a means to an end. Tell me, is that why I'm carrying your baby? Did you feel you had to trap me, force me into a corner and that I'd somehow let you get ahold of the painting then? Is that why you married me? Why you used my love for you against me?" Tears fell unchecked down her cheeks.

"Listen to yourself, Avery. You're talking crazy. Of course I didn't entrap you." Marcus shoved a hand through his hair. A hand that to Avery's stunned surprise was shaking. "Sure, I went to London to try to persuade you to part with the collection. Yes, I am Kathleen O'Reilly's great-grandson and, yes, I did want to buy the painting back. Yes, I was frustrated when you wouldn't agree to let it go. But it's not what you think. I didn't deliberately get you pregnant to make you marry me so I could get the painting."

"So you're saying that when we found out I was pregnant that the thought never even crossed your mind?" Her eyes bored into his and she could see the damning truth there. "I'm booked on the 11:00 p.m. flight back to London and I'll be instructing my lawyer to start divorce proceedings as soon as I land."

"Avery, please, don't do this," he implored.

"Goodbye, Marcus."

Fourteen

He wanted to follow her right now more than he even wanted to draw another breath—to halt her in her tracks, to drag her back to his apartment and convince her that it hadn't all been a lie. To tell her he loved her. But the rational side of him knew that she wouldn't believe him. In fact she'd probably throw his declaration straight back in his face and accuse him of continuing to try to manipulate her.

And he had manipulated her in the beginning. It was an ugly and unpalatable truth. He'd seen her attraction to him right from the start and he had lacked the scruples to simply walk away, especially once she'd shown him the painting.

That said, his own growing feelings for her had been genuine, he knew that now. He'd tried to ignore them, but love had inveigled its way through the shell he'd worn about him for so long. A shell he'd believed to be stronger than it was, when in truth it—no, *he*—was as vulnerable as the next person. And now the woman to whom he was that vulnerable man had walked away from him, carrying their child within her.

Chasing after Avery right now would be futile. She was hurting too much inside, and the knowledge that he'd caused that hurt cut him deeply. Beneath her hurt, though, he'd sensed her anger. Anger she'd had every right to feel. So he'd give her some space, for now.

It wouldn't be forever, though—he wasn't about to give up. Eventually she'd have to see him, or at least talk to him—if only to update him on her pregnancy and the birth of their baby. He knew he'd eventually have access to their son or daughter, but that was a long way off and he wanted access now. Access to Avery and to a chance to start their marriage anew. This time to start it on the right footing.

Frustration saw him swear a blue streak. There was little to nothing he could do now. He'd made his bed, as his Grampa was fond of saying, now he had to lie in it. Damn his stupid pride, Marcus thought as he paced the living-room floor for what felt like the hundredth time. He should have told Avery why he'd wanted the painting so much, why he owed his grandfather so much. But he couldn't. He simply couldn't admit out loud that it was all his fault his grandfather had sold the painting in the first place.

Even though he'd said to her that his past was not who he was now, in many ways it was. Logically he knew he hadn't made a choice to be born to parents who lacked even the basic human goodness to care for their only son, but deep down he felt responsible. If it hadn't been for him, his grandfather would still have *Lovely Woman* today.

The Price family had never had riches, certainly not the kind of riches the Cullens had taken for granted all their privileged lives. But they'd had one another. One another and a link to the past, to family, with the painting. With that gone, their final link had been severed.

The canvas had become a symbol to Marcus of all that his family had sacrificed. Kathleen sacrificed her integrity, her job and her family's security—all because a wealthy man had

ound her beautiful. Grampa had sacrificed the one thing he
ad of any genuine value—all for Marcus. Was it so bad to
ave wanted to return the picture to his grandfather?

It must have been. Because now Marcus had paid the ul-
imate price himself. He'd lost the woman he loved. But he
efused to believe it was forever. He hadn't gotten where he
vas now by letting fear of failure hold him back. He knew
ow to get what he wanted, he always had, and he wasn't
fraid to work hard for it.

Somehow, he had to prove to Avery that he was worth tak-
ng a chance on. That *Lovely Woman* didn't even factor into
is feelings for her. He thought back to the one thing, the only
hing, she'd ever asked of him—to find her angel statue. In
he excitement of returning to New York and discovering she
vas pregnant he'd let his leads run cold.

He'd failed Avery on so many levels and failure wasn't
omething that sat comfortably upon his shoulders. He had
o find the statue and return it to her so she could believe he
ad done it for her, and for her alone. Maybe then she'd be-
ieve him when he told her he loved her.

Marcus retrieved his laptop from its case and went to work.
Vork had always been his age-old panacea. It was proven—
or what he put in, he'd get something out. It was something
e could draw upon no matter what.

When he finally took a rest, he noticed daylight had begun
o break. Weariness dragged at every muscle and fiber in his
ody and he was no closer to finding the current owner of the
ngel statue. He looked at the time. Avery's flight would be
etting into London by now. Knowing she was so far away
nade the distance between them a physical pain, but some-
ow he had to work through it. Somehow he had to drive him-
elf to function, to do what he had to do to get her back—he
ould not fail. Not in this.

He went through to the bathroom and jerked on the shower
aucets, letting steam fill the air as he stripped himself of his

clothing. Would she go home first and rest? he wondered. O
would she go straight to her lawyer and put in motion the en
of everything he now held vitally dear to him?

Marcus stepped into the shower stall, closing his eyes a
he stood under the pounding deluge of water. Then and onl
then did he finally give in to the overwhelming ache in hi
chest, and let go of the sob that had been building insid
from the moment his front door had banged closed behin
her. Tears mingled with the water running down his cheek:
Tears for his family—his lost and misguided mother, his ju:
and honorable grandfather—and tears for his own stupidit
in destroying the one thing he'd thought never to have in hi
life. The unequivocal love of the woman he loved equally an
unmistakably in return.

Waverly's was quiet when he let himself in. Only one o
fice appeared to be occupied, Ann Richardson's. He didn'
feel like talking to anyone right now so he turned in the othe
direction and headed for his office. He hadn't been at his des
long when he heard a gentle knock at his door.

"Marcus? Is that you? I thought I saw you come in," An
said, letting herself in and settling into the chair opposit
him. "You're in early. What does your new wife have to sa
about that? Congratulations by the way, I'm sorry I couldn
make the ceremony on Saturday."

Marcus shot her a weak smile. "Work to do, you know hov
it is." He couldn't speak to her about what had happened wit
Avery last night. It was still too raw. He deflected the focus c
conversation off himself. "Did you even go home last night?

She laughed, a self-deprecating chuckle. "Fair call, an
for the record, yes, I did go home last night. Speaking of la:
night, how did dinner go?"

"The food was great," he commented, saying more wit
what he'd left unsaid.

Ann sat back in the chair, and waited for him to tell her what he imagined she'd really come to hear.

Marcus continued. "There's something about him… I can't quite put my finger on it, but I don't trust him. He offered me a job with Rothschild's. I expect you probably already guessed that was his intention."

"Was it a good offer?" she asked.

"It was a great offer. I didn't take it, of course."

"Of course." She smiled but the action lacked any warmth. "Thank you for your loyalty, Marcus. It won't go unrewarded. I know you're hoping for a partnership and you've earned the right to expect that. Just let us get through the next few months."

"Whatever it takes, Ann. I'm not in a hurry to go anywhere else." He sighed inwardly, wondering how much of Dalton's discussion he should share with her. It was probably only fair that she know the kind of scurrilous rumors he was spreading. "Watch your back with Rothschild, Ann. He's got a lot to say about you, and none of it's good."

"I suppose he's still beating that drum about the alleged collusion?"

"That, and the situation with the Gold Heart statue. We're certain it's not stolen property?"

Ann's mouth drew into a straight line. "Roark has never let me down before. He wouldn't have done so now."

"You hope."

"Yes, I hope." She shook her head. "No, I *know* he hasn't. Everything will turn out all right. We just have to be patient."

She rose to leave and Marcus was struck by the physical similarities between his boss and Avery. Both tall, both slender, both blonde and beautiful. Even their eyes were a similar blue, but that's where their resemblance began and ended. While Ann was an undeniably attractive woman, and he had the deepest respect for her, she had never appealed to him physically. There was little vulnerability about Ann, at least not that he'd ever noticed before, and it was the vulnerability about Avery that had drawn him so inexorably toward her.

He realized it was also that vulnerability that had made him think she was weak, that she needed his strength and protection. But he could see she had strength in full measure. It was that strength that had seen her walk away from him. It was that strength that would take care of her right now.

Perhaps that was part of his problem, Marcus conceded. His inherent need to be a knight in shining armor, slaying dragons for everyone else—but himself. Not ever wanting to acknowledge the things that could, and did, hurt him. It may be wrong of him, but that need to protect was what made him decide that his boss deserved all the support she could get. He may have hopelessly let down one of the women in his life; he was not about to do the same to the other.

"Let me know if there's any more I can do, Ann."

"Thanks, Marcus," she said with a half smile that didn't quite negate the worry in her eyes.

Avery's eyes burned with exhaustion as her cab pulled up outside her home. She felt as if she'd aged seven years, not just seven days since she'd last been here. She'd called her lawyer's office the moment her flight had landed but had been thwarted when she'd been told he was out of the office all day. She hadn't left a message or asked to speak with anyone else. Her stupidity was still too painful a reality for her to be comfortable giving that information to anyone else.

"Come on in, you poor love. I have your room all ready for you."

Mrs. Jackson's comforting chatter washed over her with the long-standing ease of familiarity and she allowed the older woman to guide her up to her room, help her undress and put her to bed. But, despite not being able to sleep on the flight, Avery could only lie on her bed, her body rigid with tension, her eyes staring unseeingly at the molded-plaster ceiling.

After an hour she couldn't take it any longer. She rose and pulled on a pair of faded blue jeans and a long-sleeved sweater and went down to the garden.

The place looked beautiful. Ted had worked a miracle. But although she could appreciate the hard work he'd put into setting the garden back to rights, back to how her father had loved it, she took little joy in its splendor.

"I didn't expect to see you back so soon," Ted said, coming around the side of the house to stand beside her. "But I'm glad I can say goodbye in person."

"Nor did I," Avery said, her voice flat. She turned to face him. "Thank you so much for all your work here. I know you said from the beginning that you'd only stay a month, but is there any chance I can change your mind? You've done a marvelous job. I'd love it if you could stay on."

"It was a delight, thank *you* for entrusting it to me. As lovely as it was, I think it's time I headed homeward soon. Folks will be needing me there."

"I'd be happy to give you a reference if you need one."

"Thank you, but, no. I won't be needing one." Ted gave her a searching look, his gaze dropping to her left hand. "That's a mighty pretty set of baubles you're wearing there. Congratulations."

Avery tried to tug the rings off her finger, but her hands had swollen slightly during the flight and hadn't settled back down. "Don't bother congratulating me," she said as she tried to work the set off. "It was a mistake."

"A mistake? Marrying someone is a pretty big step. You wouldn't have done that without thinking about it."

"That's the problem," she said, a sob rising in her throat. "I didn't think."

"There, there now," Ted comforted, patting her awkwardly on her shoulder as he led her to a bench and sat her down. "Tell me all about it."

Before she could stop herself she heard the words babbling

from her lips—everything. How she'd been attracted to Marcus from the start, how she'd known she was falling in love with him. How he'd been so obsessed with *Lovely Woman* and then the awful truth about discovering his relationship to the painting and how he'd used her to get joint ownership of it.

"You know," Ted said gently as she continued to sob beside him on the bench, "while Price might have sought you out to further his career, and to get the painting, I have no doubt the man loves you dearly. Working here in the garden gave me a chance to watch him, and to watch the two of you together. He fought it, yep, he really did. But he couldn't stop himself from loving you."

"Loving me? No, you're mistaken. The only thing he loves is that canvas up in my studio," Avery responded bitterly.

Deep down, though, she wanted Ted's words to be true. But Marcus's actions, the very words from his own lips when she'd accused him of using her, made such a hope ridiculously impossible.

"I'm sorry, Avery. Really sorry. But I think you should give the man another chance."

"I don't know if I can," she whispered.

"Look into your heart," Ted said. "You'll find the answer there. Well," he said with a sigh, "my work here is done. Remember what I said. Give him another chance. He's worth it—and so are you."

The next morning Marcus slept through his alarm. He had been up all night again, calling collectors the world over for any news of Avery's angel, eventually hitting the sheets somewhere around 3:00 a.m. He'd thought he was close at one point, but as it had so many times before, the trail had been a false one. He was seething with frustration as he made his way toward his office.

"You can't just leave that in there!" Lynette's voice filtered down the hall, the outrage in her tone a bittersweet reminder

f Mrs. Jackson's indignation that first time he'd gone to Av-
ry's house. God help him if the two women ever got together!

"What's going on?" he asked, coming around the corner
o see Lynette standing in his office doorway, her body rigid
vith irritation.

"I tried to stop them, Mr. Price. I told them and told them,
ems need to be inventoried in the storerooms downstairs
nd that they're not supposed to come to the seventh floor."

"Just following orders, miss," said the guy who was obvi-
usly senior to his partner as they maneuvered a large pack-
ng crate, about six feet high and equally as deep, off a low
urney and onto the floor at one side of Marcus's office. "Are
ou Marcus Price?"

"I am. Show me those orders," Marcus commanded, step-
ing around his PA and into the office.

The spokesman for the pair of deliverymen handed Mar-
us a sheet of paper and pointed a grubby finger at the clearly
pecified delivery instructions. *URGENT. To be delivered
ersonally to Marcus Price.* He then keyed a few digits on
ne electronic device he pulled from his belt and requested
Marcus's digital signature on the screen. Bemused, Marcus
id as requested.

"This is highly irregular, Mr. Price. We really must be
een to follow procedure," Lynette sputtered in the doorway
s the two men shuffled past her.

"I agree, but let's see what it is first, hmm?"

"You'll be needing this, then." Lynette disappeared from
ne doorway for a moment then returned, passing him a long
lim crowbar.

Marcus raised his eyebrows at her. "You keep this in your
esk?" At her nod he replied, "Remind me not to make you
iad."

"Just open the crate," she said.

The sides of the crate squealed in protest as Marcus pried
nem loose, nail by nail. He pulled away the packaging in-

side, strewing it across his office floor as, when the shape of the contents began to become clear, an unexpected excitement lit inside him.

"Oh, my, isn't she a beauty?" Lynnette commented, stepping forward to touch the pale marble face of the winged angel.

Avery's angel.

Marcus couldn't move. All he could do was stare in disbelief. For weeks he'd tried to find it, and now here it was in his office. He grabbed the sheet of paper the deliverymen had left with him, searching it for some identifying address as to its origin. But there was nothing.

"Lynnette, call the delivery company and find out where this came from," he instructed, his eyes once more glued to the serene beauty of the angel.

She was back in a moment. "No details, I'm sorry."

"That can't be right. In this day and age? To ship something this valuable without a full manifesto detailing where and who it came from?"

Lynette just shrugged. "Apparently so."

"But, why?" Marcus mused out loud.

"Maybe this will give you some idea," his PA said, stepping forward and pulling a white envelope with Marcus' name on the front from behind the wing of the statue. "It was taped on," she said, passing him the envelope.

The handwriting gave no clue as to who had penned his name with such bold black strokes of a pen. Marcus ripped the envelope open and pulled out the single sheet from inside.

My wedding gift... My work here is done. —the gardener.

"Who's the gardener?" Lynnette asked, unashamedly reading the note over Marcus's shoulder.

"I don't know," Marcus said, although something plucked at the back of his mind.

The only gardener he knew of was the man who'd been t

lying up Avery's garden. Surely someone like him wouldn't have had access to something like this? At least not legally.

Marcus racked his memory. What was the guy's name? Ted something…Wells, that was right. Ted Wells. Avery had met him through some discussion board. Which begged the question, if the guy knew Avery was looking for the statue and had obviously known where the angel statue was all along, why had he kept it from her all this time?

Fifteen

Avery stood at her studio windows, staring at the light driz-
zle that fell steadily outside. Its cool gray emptiness was th
perfect metaphor for how she felt right now. Colorless, lack
ing substance and with no clear lines marking a beginning c
end to the confusion and unhappiness that dwelt deep insid
her. She'd been home for three whole days and still she'd bee
unable to shake Ted Wells's words from her mind.

Give him another chance, Ted had urged.

A part of her wanted to do just that, but another—the pa
that still throbbed painfully with the knowledge that he'd use
her—held firm and unforgiving. It was one betrayal too man

Her hand fluttered to her belly. The life inside, mere cell
replicating, an integral part of her already. And a part c
Marcus, as well.

Would their baby be like him? Would it be an eternal to
ment to look upon their child and perhaps see Marcus's eye
looking back at her? She turned and walked over to her ease

The oil she'd done of Marcus was still lying against it as she'd left it after his final sitting.

She tried to consider the piece with a critical eye, considering whether or not to simply reduce the canvas to a blank sheet once more, but the ache in her chest at the thought of painting over his likeness, of making it as if he'd never been here, impossible. She loved Marcus, and she wanted the hurt to go away, but she didn't think she could trust him now. Especially not knowing that he'd deliberately kept his real reasons for coming here to himself even when they married.

Avery twisted her rings around on her finger. Her fingers had settled down again, back to their usual slenderness and she could have taken the rings off at any time. Yet every time she thought about it she felt his loss just that much deeper. Now, it forced her to face the truth. She didn't want to be without him. He was the father of her baby, the man she loved as she'd loved no other. Was it possible they could ever consider trying anew together? Could they build the kind of marriage her parents had enjoyed until her mother's illness had stolen her life from them?

She imagined living a half life, as her father had done for all those years after her mother had died. A half life without Marcus at her side. No wonder her father had never remarried. He'd loved once, deeply, forever—as Avery loved Marcus. She was more her father's daughter than she'd ever imagined. Right now she couldn't even begin to imagine entrusting her heart to another person. No wonder her father had never been able to do the same.

Suddenly she couldn't bear to look at the painting any longer. She turned and left the studio. Mrs. Jackson was looking for her downstairs.

"There's a delivery truck at the gates," she said, coming to meet Avery as she reached the bottom of the stairs. "They say they have a consignment for you, from New York."

"I'm not expecting anything, did they give you any de
tails?"

"No, but they insist they have all the correct paperwor
for you to sign."

"We'd better let them in, then, but ask them to bring m
the paperwork before they unload," Avery said, her curios
ity tempered with caution. The only person who'd be send
ing her anything from New York would be Marcus. So wha
was he up to? she wondered.

When Mrs. Jackson brought her the paperwork she felt a
unexpected surge of fury.

Marble Angel Statue, circa 1900.

"How dare he?" she fumed. Did he think he could buy
her off with some replica of her angel? Did he imagine fo
one second that she could be fooled into accepting anythin
but the original?

She stormed off, looking for Mrs. Jackson so she could tel
the deliverymen they could take their darned consignmen
and deliver it right back where it came from. To her horror
she saw them through the French doors leading onto the ter
race. They were in the garden already, and the sides of th
crate were being removed. She flew through the doors and
across the terrace.

"Don't—" she started to shout but whatever she was abou
to say next died in her throat as she saw what was inside th
crate.

"I never thought I'd see the day," Mrs. Jackson said as sh
sniffed, tears unashamedly trickling over her rounded cheeks
"Isn't she beautiful? She's finally back where she belongs."

Avery sank to her knees, oblivious to the moisture o
the grass soaking through the denim of her jeans. She coul
barely believe her eyes as the team who'd come with the de
livery truck and a portable crane, lifted the angel from th
crate and back onto the empty plinth where she'd resided s
many years ago.

As if to lend its seal of approval, the sun broke through the clouds, gilding the marble with its warm glow. Around her, the delivery crew gathered together all their paraphernalia and tools and withdrew. Avery was vaguely aware of the sound of the truck leaving the property but she still couldn't take her eyes from the statue.

"Look at you," Mrs. Jackson chastised, "you're getting yourself all soaked there in the grass. Come on inside."

Avery accepted the hand Mrs. Jackson offered to draw her to her feet. "I think I'll just stay out here awhile longer. I can't quite believe she's really here."

The housekeeper went back inside the house, her tsking audible for most of the way back to the terrace, but Avery didn't care. Her hands traced the lines of the angel's wings, her flowing gown, her graceful slender arms.

"You're back," Avery whispered. "He found you and brought you back to me."

It was easy to fall into old patterns and to settle at the foot of the angel and begin to open up her heart as she'd done so many times as a lonely child. And, as she did so, Avery could feel the weight upon her chest lifting.

"I miss him, I miss him so much. But I don't know if I can ever trust him again," she ended softly, after pouring her sorrow out from where it had been dammed up since she'd walked out on the only man she'd ever loved.

"Try, Avery. Please, will you give me another chance?"

She stiffened and turned, rising to her feet when she saw the man standing there. She blinked, as if she didn't quite believe her eyes.

"What are you doing here?" she asked, her voice strained.

Instead of answering her immediately, Marcus gave her a sheet of paper. She opened it, reading its contents in seconds.

"His wedding gift? What—?" Confusion made her mind spin. "This is from Ted? *He* gave us the statue as a wedding gift?"

"It seems weird, doesn't it?" Marcus agreed. "I wish
could have been the one to find it for you, but I guess th
most important thing is that she's back where she belongs
She looks good there. As if she never left."

"But…why? Why would he do this? And to call it a wed
ding gift?"

Marcus shrugged. "Maybe he thought we deserved an
other chance at this marriage of ours. I know I do. I want u
to make this work, Avery."

She half turned away, biting her lip. "I…I don't know
Marcus. We rushed into everything, never thought any of i
through. And I still feel used—lied to."

"I know, and I'm so sorry. I wish I had been open wit
you right from the start. Told you everything up-front." Hi
voice broke, the wretched sound making her face him agair

"Avery, I love you. I love you more than anything or any
one else in the world. You are my everything and I don't wan
to live the rest of my life regretting that I didn't make mor
of an effort to convince you to take another chance on me
Please, give me, give *us,* another chance."

"I'm scared," she admitted. "You hurt me so badly. I don'
want to be that vulnerable again. Ever."

"But isn't that part of loving another person? Making your
self vulnerable to them? Don't you think I feel vulnerabl
here, now, standing before you, knowing you hold my futur
happiness in your hands?"

He reached out, taking her hands in his and holding then
to his chest. Beneath her palms Avery felt the warmth of hi
body seeping into her cooler skin, felt the beat of his hear
and wanted to believe that it beat for her. Wanted it with
longing that reached to the depths of her soul.

"I do? Do I have that power over you?" she whispered.

"And more. I was a single-minded fool. And I was wron
when I told you that my past is not who I am. My past is ev
erything about who I am now. It formed me, gave me a pu

ose. Everything. I just didn't know, until it was too late, that ometimes you have to vary from the road you've carved out or yourself if you truly want to be happy."

Marcus rested his forehead against hers briefly before continuing. "You know a bit about my background, about how my parents were junkies. For some crazy reason my mother oved my father enough to walk away from everything she'd ever known, from all the security my grandfather had worked hard to provide for her, and all to throw her life away on a man who let her take the fall for him when their apartment was raided. She was sent away, to serve a sentence that he should have been given. And he kept her supplied the whole time. When I was born, social services tracked down my grandfather who took me in. Until they knocked on his door he didn't even know he had a grandson. I was two when the police notified him that my mother had died of an overdose—he was devastated. I think he'd hoped deep down, that if she knew he had me, that one day she'd come back home. Pick up her life again when she got out.

"But it seemed she couldn't stand a life without my father. After Grampa had buried her, he thought that would be an end to it, but my father found him. He came to the house threatening to take me away. Grampa offered him money, a whole lot of money, if my father would walk away forever. My father accepted and that's when Grampa sold *Lovely Woman*. He said it was worth it, but all my life I knew he'd done it because of me."

"But, Marcus, that was his choice. He could have fought for your custody in court. No judge would ever have allowed your father to take you, given his background."

"Grampa wasn't prepared to take the risk. He had a friend who was a lawyer write up an agreement and he made my father sign it before handing over the money. I was twelve when Grampa told me the whole story, and I promised myself that day that when I was old enough I would buy *Lovely Woman* back for him. It was the only thing he had left of his mother and he'd let it go to keep me. I owed it to him."

Avery felt tears burn her eyes for the passionate and determined boy Marcus had been. And for the passionate and determined man now standing before her.

"I understand," she said softly.

His hands tightened on hers. "Do you? Do you see why I was so blind to everything else that I made the most stupid mistake of my life in trying to use you? Can you forgive me that mistake, Avery?"

She lifted one hand to cup his cheek and looked deep into his eyes. "I can, Marcus, and I do. I left you because I was afraid you were just like everyone else who ever used me in the past. Whether it was for money, or contacts, or just to say they knew me, people have walked all over me all my life. Yes, I'm lucky enough to have a handful of true friends, but it's been a hard road finding those gems amongst the fakes. I was too quick to paint you with the same brush."

"You were justified in doing so," he said before turning his face so he could kiss the palm of her hand.

The heat of his lips sent a gentle thread of warmth to unfurl through her body—a warmth she realized she had been lacking since she'd left New York.

"Maybe so, but I didn't want to listen to you in New York. I just wanted to leave, so I did."

"You were right to go. I had been using you, I admit that, and I did realize that our assets became joint with our marriage. But that wasn't why I married you. I asked you before I even realized it myself, but, Avery, you have to believe me. When I said my vows to you last Saturday, I was saying them from the heart. I love you with every breath in my body, every beat of my heart."

"You were so distant after the wedding, I started to second guess everything. I worried that you'd married me just to get a hold of *Lovely Woman* and then when I saw Peter and

he told me exactly who she was… Well, it all just made too
much horrible sense."

"I was a fool. I'd rushed you into getting married when
we should have enjoyed taking our time toward planning the
rest of our lives together. It would have given me a chance to
show you how much I love you, to make you believe it, before we tied the knot."

She gave a broken little laugh. "I didn't exactly protest
about our wedding being so soon, Marcus."

He smiled back at her and she felt her heart swell with the
knowledge it was genuine and just for her.

"No, you didn't, did you?" Marcus bent and kissed her
sweetly. "I'm glad. But I'm not letting you go. Not now I
have you. You've taught me so much about love. I thought I
knew it all. Grampa and I, we have a bond that nothing will
break and I thought that was all that love could be. Through
you, though, I've learned that it can be so much more. I never
knew what it was like to be truly loved by a woman, a life
partner—someone who loves me wholly and unconditionally
by choice, not by an accident of birth.

"We didn't take time to get to know one another, but if
you're prepared to give us another try, give our love and our
marriage another chance, then so am I."

Avery reached up to pull his face down to hers. Against
his lips she said, "I'd like that very much."

Sixteen

It was late the next morning when Marcus awoke. For a moment, when he reached for Avery and found her gone from their bed where they'd made the sweetest love he'd ever experienced in his whole life, he felt a pang of fear and loss all over again. But almost as quickly as the alarm flooded his consciousness, she was there at the bedroom door.

"Come here, you," he growled, patting the bed beside him.

"Not just yet." She smiled. "Here, I have something for you. A belated wedding gift."

He saw the wrapped rectangle and knew it instantly. It had to be the nude she'd completed of him before they'd gone to New York. Eager to see her expertise again, he ripped away the paper, but instead of the unframed canvas he'd been expecting, his hands unveiled the familiar and graceful form of his great-grandmother.

"I want you to have it," she said in response to the unasked question that hovered on his lips.

"Avery, you didn't have to do this," he said, his voice rough with emotion. "You're the only lovely woman I need, now or ever."

"Then give it to your Grampa. Seriously. I want him to have it if you won't."

He leaned the painting against the side of the bed and reached for her, wrapping her in his arms, and showed his thanks the most eloquent way he knew how.

The sun was almost at its zenith when they rose from their bed, as they did, Marcus noticed the painting had fallen from where he'd propped it earlier on. Cursing himself for his carelessness he reached to pick it up.

"Damn," he muttered, noticing that the back of the painting appeared to have popped away from the frame slightly.

"What's wrong?" Avery asked, dragging a robe around her naked body.

"I knocked this over and look—" he gestured to the back "—I've damaged it."

"Here, let me see," Avery answered, taking the picture from him. "That's strange, it looks like there's something in there, wedged between the canvas and the backing."

She went to her dressing table and grabbed a pair of manicure scissors.

"What are you doing?"

"Don't worry, we can get it repaired. I have contacts you know," she teased gently. "But what is this—"

Marcus leaned forward as she pried the back loose. "It looks like an envelope."

Avery picked up the yellow vellum packet and read the front, "Miss Kathleen O'Reilly. Do you think it's from Baxter?"

"Only one way to find out."

He slid his finger under the fold of the envelope, breaking the seal and then carefully extracted the thick sheaf of papers inside. "These look like stock certificates, and look, there's a letter."

"My dearest Kathleen," Avery read. *"It is with a sad-dened heart I forward this to you. I love you, my darling girl, I always will, but I cannot leave my wife—the scandal will destroy our children, our families. I was wrong to take advan-tage of you, wrong to let you love me, but I will always hold your love deep inside my heart, until my dying day. While I cannot be your husband, as I truly wish, I can at least pro-vide for you and your family and I hope the stock certificates can make a difference for your life now, and for the future. –Yours, always, Baxter C."*

"He did love her," Marcus said, struggling to believe what he'd just heard. "You know, I always thought he just used her then let his wife throw her out without giving her another thought, but he tried to make amends. He really did try. Now I know what the original note he sent with the painting meant. My grandfather still has it."

"What did it say?" Avery asked, picking up the stock cer-tificates and studying them carefully.

"It's what's inside that counts. Obviously the reference was too literal for Kathleen. She always told my grandfather that it had to do with the painting itself. She could have sold it at any time, but she always held on to it. Whether as a reminder of a love lost, or as a reminder of what her family called her biggest mistake, she couldn't let it go. It's part of what drove me so hard to get it back when I learned why Grampa sold it—knowing she could have made money from it all those years ago. Baxter Cullen was already well-known. If she'd sold it back then it would have given her family a financial boost they dearly needed."

"I'd like to think she kept it because she loved him, and because in her heart she knew he loved her. But, Marcus—" Avery waved the stock certificates toward him "—if you want to talk about financial boosts, I think you should look at these. They're worth millions now. I'm not kidding. Millions. Your grandfather is now a very wealthy man."

Marcus took the certificates from her and pored over them. He couldn't believe his eyes. All those years Kathleen had suffered and worked her fingers raw and she'd never known about the security that Baxter had given her. "If only she'd understood," Marcus said softly.

Avery put her hand over his, squeezing his fingers reassuringly. "You know, I'm sorry that your family had life so hard through the years. It could all have been very different for you. All of you."

"You know," Marcus said, looking up at her, "I'm not sorry. Yes, life was hard, but if it hadn't been I might never have met you, and never been able to tell you how much I love you."

"Oh, Marcus," she said, and he could see the shimmer of moisture in her eyes. "I love you, too. You're the man of my dreams. Today, tomorrow and for always."

* * * * *

*Turn the page
for a special bonus story
by* USA TODAY *bestselling author
Barbara Dunlop.
Then look for the next installment
of* THE HIGHEST BIDDER,
*A PRECIOUS INHERITANCE,
by Paula Roe.
Wherever Harlequin Books are sold.*

THE GOLD HEART, PART 3
Barbara Dunlop

Kalila Khouri gaped in astonishment at her new British roommate, Alexis Payton. In their two-bed dorm room at Rushmore House on the campus of Rayard International School in Istanbul, the willowy, blond-haired, blue-eyed Alexis shimmied out of her silver-and-black spandex top to reveal a lacy purple bra.

"Is it true what they say?" asked Alexis, tossing the top onto one of the beds and snapping her bright green gum between her teeth. "Are you really a princess?"

Kalila nodded, quite literally speechless. Never mind the avant-garde clothing, nobody had ever undressed in front of her before.

"That's so cool," said Alexis. She rummaged through one of two matching plaid suitcases, retrieving another slinky top, this one bright pink. "My parents own factories in Birmingham. Well, also in China and India. But we brag mor about Birmingham."

She pulled the top over her head, adjusting the loose scoped collar and cap sleeves. Then she tugged the fabri over her hips, unsnapping the top of her black jeans. She sli them off, and Kalila realized the pink garment was a dress not a shirt.

The jeans followed the spandex top into a heap on the bed and the hem of the dress settled high on Alexis's thighs. Then it got worse. Alexis unsnapped her bra, wriggling around unti she tugged it out one of the sleeves, and discarded it with th rest of her clothes.

"There," she breathed, fluffing her wavy hair. "I'm set So, what are you going to wear?"

Kalila glanced down at her sarong-style, mauve silk dress It covered her arms to the wrists, and the skirt draped all th way to her ankles. The fabric was airy, the embroidery made i pretty and the wide sash at the waist was quite fashionable i her home country. "Is there something wrong with my dress?"

"No, no." Alexis quickly rushed forward. "It's very pretty But…" Her lips pinched together. "The guys from Hamil ton Hall are throwing a party at a neighborhood club. Yo know, a welcome to Istanbul and the Rayard school-year bash You'll…"

Kalila's stomach clenched as Alexis obviously struggle for kind words.

"I'm afraid you'll stand out, is all," Alexis finished. "Be cause that gown makes you look…uh, so incredibly pretty."

Despite her embarrassment, Kalila couldn't help a grin "Why do I get the sense that 'pretty' is a euphemism?"

Alexis gave a relieved smile in return. "Your English i better than mine."

"I learned it as a child."

Her uncle King Safwah had recognized English as th language of commerce, and he'd set about giving the roya princes an advantage in life. As a princess, Kalila had mostly been to be married to her.

"I didn't mean to insult your dress." There was genuine concern in Alexis's eyes.

"You have me worried," Kalila admitted, glancing down.

She didn't want to stand out amongst her classmates. Though it was customary now for the male members of the Rayas royal family to take some of their education abroad, that option had never been open to the girls, until Kalila.

She wanted to make the most of her year, because, in June, she would be summoned back to the palace, where she would marry Ari Alber, the son of an important sheikh, a man twenty years older than her.

"Go ahead," she told Alexis bravely. "Tell me what's wrong."

Alexis squinted. "It's too, too..." She lifted the wide sleeves, fingering the fabric of the full skirt. "Too much."

"Too long?" Kalila guessed. Though she'd seen a few other women in the Istanbul airport in full-length dresses, most had worn slacks or shorter skirts.

"Too voluminous. I can barely find you in there. Do you have anything shorter?"

Kalila shook her head. "Nobody wears short skirts in Rayas."

"What about pants?"

"I don't wear slacks."

In the international areas of the capital city, split skirts had given way in recent years to wider legged slacks for some of the young Rayas women. But the royal family was much slower to change.

Alexis pondered. "You could borrow something of mine. We're pretty close in size."

Kalila's mouth dropped open and went dry at the thought of wearing a pink, sleeveless minidress with no bra.

Her fear must have shown, because Alexis laughed.

"Nothing too radical, I promise." Alexis lifted and plunked the larger suitcase on the bed and unzipped the top.

She rummaged around for a few minutes, then held up a royal-blue satin dress. The fabric was puckered and crinkled, so it shone from all angles. "How about this? It's not too clingy."

Kalila stepped back warily. "It's way too short." And it didn't have any sleeves, just wide, blocky straps that would barely cover her shoulders.

"I've got leggings," Alexis announced, producing what looked like a pair of thin, black slacks. "Those'll cover your legs, and we can use a shawl to cover your arms. I've got some blue-suede ankle boots— What size are your feet?"

Kalila's shoes had always been custom-made. "I never thought to ask," she admitted.

Alexis raised her brows. "You've never been to a shoe store, have you?"

"Shoemakers come to the palace," Kalila admitted.

Alexis laughed as she peered at Kalila's feet. "I love it. Okay, I'm going to guess a seven. My boots should fit you."

Kalila started to protest that she couldn't possibly wear Alexis's clothes or her shoes. But Alexis was determined. And before Kalila knew what was happening, she was standing in front of the full-length mirror on the back of the room's bathroom door, staring in awe. She looked like she'd stepped out of a fashion magazine.

"You have fantastic legs," Alexis enthused.

"I can't go out like this."

"Why not? Everything's covered. But we need to do something with all that hair."

Everything was *not* covered, at least not securely. If Kalila made a wrong move, her arms would be bare. And the leggings delineated every curve of her calves and thighs. The king would fall over dead if he saw her like this. Even her cousin Raif would have a heart attack.

"I can't walk in these boots," she protested.

Though she had to admit, she liked them. They felt fun and exotic on her feet.

"Practice before we go," Alexis suggested. She moved behind Kalila, gathering her hair into a bunch and twirling it into a knot.

"Do you have any jewelry?" she asked.

"I have plenty of jewelry," Kalila affirmed. Royal Rayasan women might not be the height of Western fashion, but they knew how to accessorize.

"Well, pull it out," said Alexis.

Kalila felt strangely delighted at being about to contribute to the dress-up session.

She retrieved her traveling jewelry box, opening it five ways to display the gems she'd chosen for the trip.

Alexis stared in silence.

"What do you think?" Kalila prompted a little nervously.

"Is this all real?" Alexis reached out to tentatively touch an emerald necklace.

"It's real. Do you like it?"

"I *love* it."

Kalila warmed to the task, happy to have something to contribute in return. "Then pick something. You can borrow it." She eyed the bright pink dress and Alexis's blond hair. Then she reached in to open a smaller compartment in the box, extracting a sapphire and diamond choker. "Try this."

"Are you sure?"

"Go ahead. It'll go great with the dress."

Alexis giggled. "Okay, but then I'm doing your makeup."

"I don't wear makeup."

"I'll be subtle. Nobody will know but us. Oh, my Lord, this is stunning."

Kalila helped her with the clasp. Sure enough, the choker was perfect.

Alexis dashed to the mirror, fingering the gems as she gazed at her reflection. "We are going to have *so* much fun."

Kalila's hair was swept up in a messy knot. Alexis had applied a subtle layer of makeup that highlighted her dark eyes and accentuated her lips and cheekbones. She was still self conscious about the leggings, and was being careful to keep the shawl over her arms. But as she walked into the dark club, its colored lights flashing, techno music throbbing as dancers thumped on the floor, she realized nobody was paying the slightest bit of attention to her.

"This way," Alexis shouted in her ear above the noise, pointing. "It'll be quieter in the back."

Alexis started her way through the dense crowd, and Kalila ducked in behind, walking carefully in the high-heeled boots. After what seemed like an eternity, they passed into a quieter hallway, where couples and groups lounged against the walls, sipping brightly colored drinks, talking and laughing.

At the end of the hall, a burly security guard stood in front of a velvet rope, his meaty arms crossed over his deep chest. He frowned as they grew closer.

"Ma'am?" he said to Alexis in a deep voice.

Instead of answering, she focused on a point past him. "Hey, Niles," she called, giving a wave.

A man looked up from where he sat in a furniture grouping. He was maybe twenty, incredibly handsome, with a square chin, straight nose, a thick shock of ginger hair and a pair of startlingly deep blue eyes that flashed when he caught sight of Alexis. As he stood, his three friends followed his gaze.

"Lexi," he called.

He gave a subtle nod to the doorman, and the man unclipped the rope to let them in.

"How was the flight?" he asked, pulling her into a quick hug.

"Boring," Alexis replied, stepping back. "This is my new roommate, Kalila," she introduced. Then she lowered her voice to a conspiratorial level. "She's a princess."

Niles looked at Kalila with obvious curiosity.

She wished Alexis hadn't said anything about her royal status. She hoped the man wasn't intimidated by it.

She tried to compensate. "It's not…" Her brain stumbled for a moment. "I mean, you don't have to…"

But Niles's lips curved into a grin.

Alexis elbowed her playfully. "Relax. Niles is a marquess. He'll be a duke someday. He's not bothered by a princess."

Kalila felt her face heat. They were laughing at her. Why hadn't she kept her mouth shut?

He held out his hand. "Your Royal Highness—"

"You're mocking me."

"Not at all. Simply observing protocol. Niles Hammond Walden-Garv, Marquess of Vendich, at your service."

"Kalila Khouri." She shook his hand.

He raised his brow and waited, obviously wanting her to finish the title.

Fine. She'd play along. "Princess Kalila Dhelal Rashidah Khouri, House of Bajal, Rayas."

Niles kept his blue eyes focused on her, and something about his regard made her body warm. "Lila," he said softly. "Lila and Lexi. Nice."

Then the tone of his voice changed, but he didn't break eye contact with Kalila. "Lexi? You still hot for Anton?"

"I was *never* hot for Anton," Alexis retorted.

"Hey, Anton," Niles called, his blue eyes continuing to sparkle into Kalila's. She felt like she was falling under some sort of spell.

"Yeah?" one of the young men at the table responded, coming to his feet.

"Let's get out of here."

"Don't you dare," Alexis hissed.

But Niles just laughed. "You'll thank me later."

"I absolutely will not—"

Anton arrived and glanced expectantly around the group. "Where're we going?"

"Down the coast," said Niles, slipping his hand into Kalila's.

She tried to pull away, but he held her fast, and she had no choice but to start walking as he tugged her toward the exit. Alexis and Anton fell in behind. Kalila wasn't so sure they should be leaving with the two men. Then again, she definitely wasn't staying at the party without Alexis.

"The car's out front," Niles told Kalila.

Okay. That was better. It was a relief to hear his driver was waiting.

"First time in Istanbul?" he asked her.

Just then, they entered the dance room, with its throbbing music and stomping feet, so she merely nodded in response.

He said something else, but she couldn't for the life of her make out what it was. And, anyway, she was occupied with keeping her shawl in place, using only one hand.

Niles's hand was square and broad, warm and slightly callused against hers. It occurred to her this was the first time she'd ever touched a male who wasn't a relative. It should have felt strange, but it didn't.

At the other end of the room they squeezed their way past a line on the staircase, then out into the cool evening. Traffic moved up and down the street. Lights shone from storefronts and apartment buildings, and the sea stood black against a moon-bright nighttime sky.

"The yellow one," said Niles, pointing to a low-slung sports car, top down, snug up against the curb.

"Where's your driver?" she asked.

He used their joined hands to move her in an arc toward the passenger door, deftly opening it with the other.

"London," he answered. "Hop in."

She stopped, bracing her hand on the top of the open door. "We can't go alone."

"We're not going alone. Lexi and Anton are coming with us."

"There are only two seats."

He cocked his head. "That's Anton's ride behind us. They'll meet us there."

"Meet us where?"

But Alexis was already getting into the other car, and Niles snagged Kalila's elbow, propelling her into the vehicle.

"You'll love it. I promise," he vowed, closing the door tight.

He gave Anton and Alexis a jaunty wave, then rounded the back of the car and hopped in.

Kalila was even less sure now of what she was doing.

She glanced behind to Alexis, who was gesticulating at Anton, clearly making an argument of some kind. Kalila reached for the door handle to escape.

"They do that all the time," Niles drawled, pulling out into traffic. "Lexi fusses and fumes, but she truly does have the hots for him."

"The hots?" Kalila found herself asking.

"It's a colloquialism for her wanting to make out with him."

"Oh." Kalila didn't want any more details. If it was true, it was completely Alexis's business. She was British, and they did things differently there.

"I'm assuming Rayasian princesses don't make out."

"We do not," Kalila confirmed.

"Ever kissed anyone?"

"No," she answered with a lift of her chin. She would not let his impertinence unsettle her.

"You don't date?"

"I don't date." That wasn't the way things worked in Rayas, at least in royal circles.

"Even in England, there's a double standard."

"Double standard?"

"It's okay for guys to...uh, make out with girls, but girl have to worry about their reputations."

"Well, it's not okay for anyone to kiss me."

Niles chuckled. "Do they get thrown in the dungeon?"

"They'd get arrested."

He gazed at her for a long moment. Her chest tightened and a buzzing sensation radiated out from the pit of her stom ach.

"I'll keep that in mind," he said softly.

"I'm getting married," she found herself blurting out.

"Good for you," said Niles, refocusing his attention on th road and gearing down for a curve.

They passed ancient, towering mosques and stone churche interspersed with modern buildings. Crowds of people move along the sidewalks, while the sea breeze pushed the scent of jasmine and salt water over the smell of exhaust.

"Who and when?" he asked.

She turned to look at him. "Who and when, what?"

"Who are you marrying, and when are you doing it?"

"Oh. Ari Alber. Next year sometime."

"You don't sound very excited."

She wasn't. "He's older than me. The son of an importar sheikh. Quite conservative." She couldn't help a reflexiv glance at her clothing. She couldn't even imagine what Ar Alber would say if he saw her in this outfit.

She realized that her arms had come free of the shawl, an she struggled to cover them up.

"It doesn't sound as if you like him much," Niles observed

Kalila gave a shrug. "It could be worse."

Niles glanced from his driving to her, an odd expressior on his handsome face. "That's what you say about your fi ancé? It could be worse?"

"We're not engaged yet."

"Well, when he asks, maybe you should say no." Niles negotiated around a stone garden, deftly avoiding a group of pedestrians who'd strayed from the sidewalk.

"There's an understanding," she explained.

Niles went silent as the buildings turned to palm trees, and they entered a strip of parkland. "Between you and him, or between your families?"

She couldn't help but laugh at that. "Rayas is not Britain."

Niles glanced at her with that funny expression again. "How old are you, Kalila?"

"Nineteen."

"And you've never been kissed."

"I have not." As she said the words, she felt a funny shimmer cross her lips, as if they were itchy and wanted to be soothed. She couldn't help thinking of kissing Niles.

She blinked hard and gave her head a little shake.

Suddenly, he braked, taking an abrupt left turn into a beachfront parking lot. The lot was big, and poorly lit, and he swung the sports car into a corner spot, facing the ocean.

When he killed the engine, the sound of the waves took up the silence. She quickly realized that Alexis and Anton hadn't followed.

Niles turned in his seat. "You're going to marry a man you don't like, having never kissed another."

She swallowed against the sultry atmosphere pressing in from the sea. "That's not unusual."

Unexpectedly, he exited the vehicle, coming around to her side and opening the door.

Was he kicking her out? Had she said something wrong?

He stood back and waited.

She wasn't confident enough to stand her ground, so she tightened the shawl and gingerly climbed out of the seat, rising in front of him.

He gazed down at her, silhouetted by a faraway streetlamp,

his features obscured. His tone was husky. "You're a beauti
ful woman, Lila."

"That's not my name," she managed.

"Maybe not." He shifted closer. "But I've got an entire
school year to help you get used to it."

He brushed a stray lock of hair from her cheek. She knew
she should protest, that she must protest, but the words froze
in her throat. His fingertips felt incredibly good against her
skin. His voice was deep and compelling. Her gaze moved
involuntarily to his lips.

"By the end of the year," he promised in a night whisper,
"You'll love it."

She feared she might love it already.

"I want to kiss you, Lila."

"My uncle will throw you in jail."

"Your uncle's not here."

"He'll find out."

"And if he wouldn't find out?" Niles inched ever closer,
tipping his head, fingertips moving to cup her chin. "If we
knew for certain he'd never find out? If no one but me and
you would ever know, would you let me kiss you?"

It was a fascinating question.

"You're not saying no," he pointed out, easing inexora
bly closer.

He was right. She wasn't saying no. Why wasn't she say
ing no?

Then his lips touched hers, softly, gently. It was a mere
whisper, but the warmth sizzled all the way through her body.

His palm cupped her face, his lips pressing more firmly
and the sensations intensified, zipping through her blood
stream, weakening her bones.

His arm went around her waist, tugging her close, as his
lips urged hers apart. She opened to him, bracing her hands
on his shoulders, gripping tight to steady the world.

"Lila." His tone was guttural. "Tell me no."

But she couldn't speak. She didn't seem to be capable of protesting or pulling away. Instead, the shawl fluttered from her shoulders and blew off into the night.

A sneaky peek at next month...

MODERN™

INTERNATIONAL AFFAIRS, SEDUCTION & PASSION GUARANTEED

My wish list for next month's titles...

In stores from 20th September 2013:

❏ The Greek's Marriage Bargain — Sharon Kendrick

❏ The Playboy of Puerto Banús — Carol Marinelli

❏ The Divorce Party — Jennifer Hayward

❏ A Hint of Scandal — Tara Pammi

In stores from 4th October 2013:

❏ An Enticing Debt to Pay — Annie West

❏ Marriage Made of Secrets — Maya Blake

❏ Never Underestimate a Caffarelli — Melanie Milburne

❏ A Precious Inheritance — Paula Roe

Available at WHSmith, Tesco, Asda, Eason, Amazon and Apple

Just can't wait?

Visit us Online

You can buy our books online a month before they hit the shops! **www.millsandboon.co.uk**

0913/

She's loved and lost — will she ever learn to open her heart again?

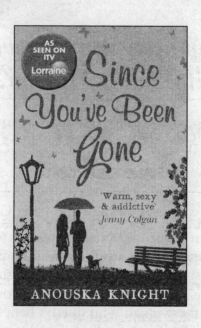

From the winner of ITV Lorraine's Racy Reads, Anouska Knight, comes a heart-warming tale of love, loss and confectionery.

'The perfect summer read — warm, sexy and addictive!'
—Jenny Colgan

For exclusive content visit:
www.millsandboon.co.uk/anouskaknight

MILLS & BOON®
Book Club

Join the Mills & Boon Book Club

Subscribe to **Modern**™ today for 3, 6 or 12 months and you could **save over £40!**

We'll also treat you to these fabulous extras:

- 🌹 **FREE L'Occitane gift set worth £10**

- 🌹 **FREE home delivery**

- 🌹 **Rewards scheme, exclusive offers…and much more!**

Subscribe now and save over £40
www.millsandboon.co.uk/subscribeme